preeto
& Other Stories

the male gaze in urdu

edited and introduced by
Rakhshanda Jalil

THORNBIRD
NIYOGI BOOKS

Published by
NIYOGI BOOKS
Block D, Building No. 77,
Okhla Industrial Area, Phase-I,
New Delhi-110 020, INDIA
Tel: 91-11-26816301, 26818960
Email: niyogibooks@gmail.com
Website: www.niyogibooksindia.com

Original Text © Authors
Translated Text © Individual translators

Editor: Gita Rajan
Cover Design: Misha Oberoi
Design: Nabanita Das

ISBN: 978-93-86906-64-9
Publication: 2018

This is a work of fiction. The names, characters and incidents portrayed in it are the work of the author's imagination. Any resemblance to actual persons, living or dead, events or localities, is entirely coincidental.

All rights are reserved. No part of this publication may be reproduced or transmitted in any form or by any means, electronic or mechanical, including photocopying, recording or by any information storage and retrieval system without prior written permission and consent of the Publisher.

Printed at: Niyogi Offset Pvt. Ltd., New Delhi, India

Dedicated to
Aaliya, Insha, Alvira and Fiza
in the hope that they will not allow themselves
to be defined by the male gaze

Contents

7
Introduction

21
Woman
Rajinder singh bedi

29
Preeto
Krishan Chandar

45
Man
Gulzar

51
Shonali
Faiyaz Riffat

61
The Wedding Night
Ratan Singh

67
The Heavy Stone
Baig Ehsas

81
Awaiting the Zephyr
Syed Muhammad Ashraf

99
Driftwood
Deepak Budki

109
The Unexpected Disaster
Hussainul Haque

131
A Bit Odd
Zamiruddin Ahmad

137
The Ash in the Fire
Abdus Samad

157
Asexual
Rahman Abbas

173
The Well of Serpents
Siddique Alam

194
Glossary

196
Notes on Contributors

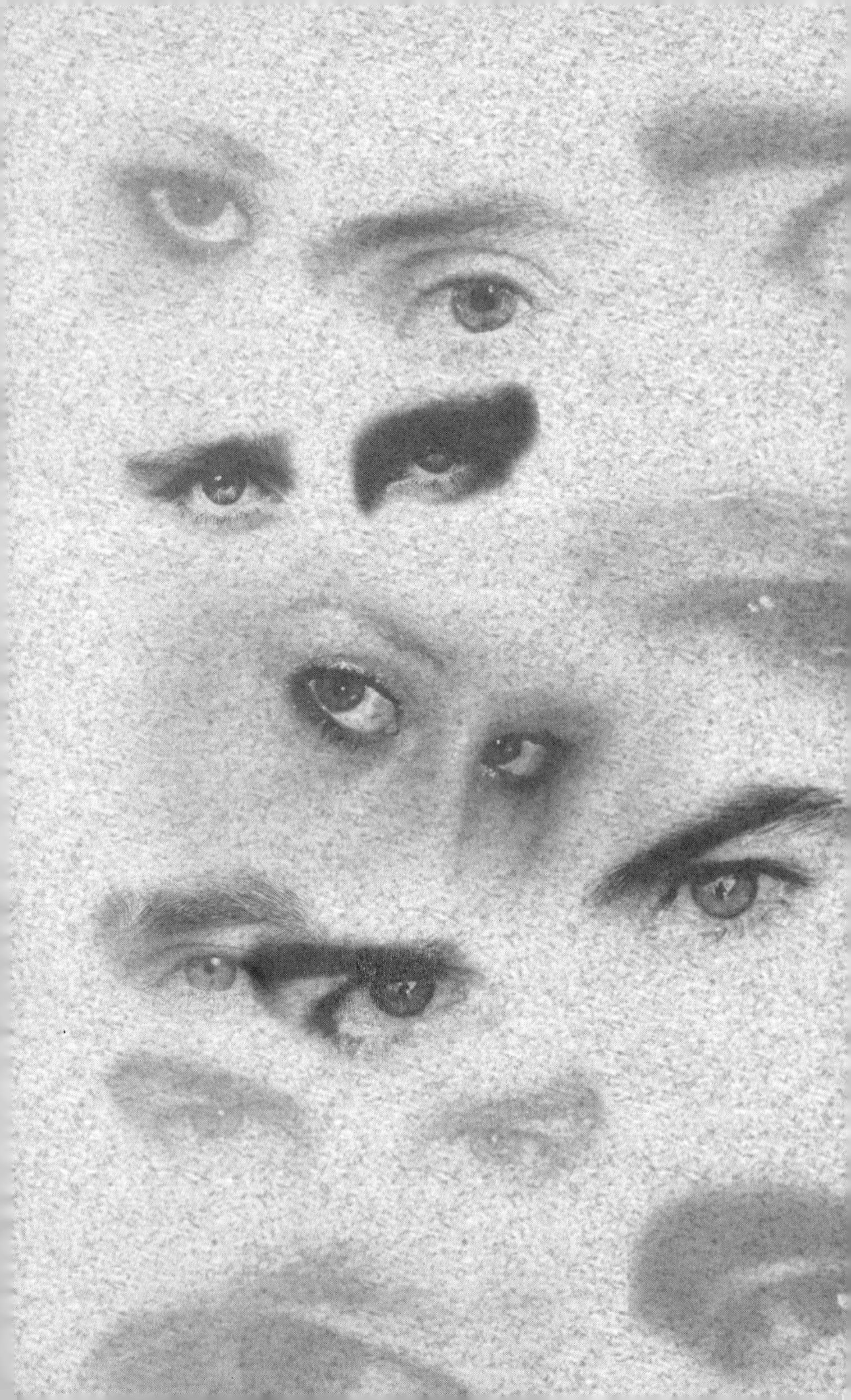

Introduction

'In a world ordered by sexual imbalance, pleasure in looking has been split between active/male and passive/female. The determining male gaze projects its fantasy on to the female form which is styled accordingly. In their traditional exhibitionist role women are simultaneously looked at and displayed, with their appearance coded for strong visual and erotic impact so that they can be said to connote to-be-looked-at-ness.'

Laura Mulvey, *Visual and Other Pleasures*

The woman has been both subject and predicate in a great deal of writing by male writers. In poetry she has, of course, been the subject of vast amounts of romantic, even sensuous imagery. Be it muse or mother, vamp or victim, fulsome or flawed, there has been a tendency among male writers to view a woman through a binary of 'this' or 'that' and to present women as black and white characters, often either impossibly white or improbably black. Since men are not expected to be one or the other but generally taken to be a combination of contraries, such a monochromatic view inevitably results in women being reduced to objects, of being taken to be 'things' rather than 'people'. That this objectification of women, and the consequent dehumanisation, effectively 'others' half the human population seems to escape many writers, even those ostensibly desirous of breaking stereotypes or those who see themselves as liberal, even emancipated men. Films, television and media have traditionally aided and abetted the idea that women are objects to be pursued and eventually won over like trophies or prizes. Literature has fed into the trope that women are bona fide objects of sexual fantasy, or blank canvases on which men can paint their ideals, or even empty vessels into which they can pour their pent-up feelings and emotions.

Feminist theoreticians would have us believe that there is, and has always been, a traditional heterosexual way of men looking at women, a way that presents women as essentially sexual objects for the pleasure of the male viewer. The feminist film critic Laura Mulvey, in her seminal essay 'Visual Pleasure and Narrative Cinema' (1975), termed this way of seeing as the 'male gaze'. Mulvey's theory was based on the premise that 'an asymmetry of power between the genders is a controlling force in cinema; and that the male gaze is constructed for the pleasure of the male viewer which is deeply rooted in the ideologies and discourses of patriarchy'. Within a short span of time, the expression slipped into accepted usage and moved seamlessly across medium: from film to literature to popular culture. Today, we use the term loosely to describe ways of men seeing women and consequently presenting or representing them.

In the context of Urdu, I have always been intrigued by how men view women and, by extension, write about them. For that matter, I am equally intrigued by how women view women and the world around them. In fact, as a precursor to this present volume, I had edited a selection of writings in Urdu by women called *Neither Night Nor Day* (Harper Collins, 2007). I had set myself a deliberately narrow framework by looking at women writers from Pakistan as I was curious to discover how women, in an essentially patriarchal society, view the place of women in the world. I chose 13 contemporary women writers and tried to examine the image and representation of women by women.

Introduction

Now, ten years later, I have attempted to do the same with male writers, except that this time I have chosen Indian writers. While I have begun with two senior writers, Rajinder Singh Bedi and Krishan Chandar, I have chosen not to go back to the early male writers such as Sajjad Hyder Yildrum, Qazi Abdul Ghaffar or even Premchand, for that matter, who wrote extensively on women. For the purpose of this study, I wanted to make a selection from modern writers. In a world where more women are joining the work force, where ever more are stepping out from their secluded and cloistered world and can be physically seen in larger numbers, I was curious to see how, then, do male writers view and consequently present or represent the women of their world.

But before we come to my selection from the present times, it might be useful to understand the literary world contemporary Urdu writers have inherited and how women have been represented in Urdu fiction in the hands of the masters.

The Woman in Urdu Short Fiction

The four pillars of the Urdu short story — Saadat Hasan Manto, Ismat Chughtai, Rajinder Singh Bedi and Krishan Chandar — are not merely the finest exponents of the genre but can also be credited with introducing a realistic portrayal of women in Urdu fiction. Their women are a far cry from the cosmetic, unnatural, almost fictionalised depictions of women that Urdu readers had hitherto encountered.

Saadat Hasan Manto was among the earliest Urdu writers to have written about women with any degree of naturalness. He wrote about women in a way that no other writer from the Indian sub-continent had or has, till today. *Sadak ke Kinare* ('By the Roadside') was a beautiful elegy to a mother forced to abandon her baby. Here Manto, quite literally, got under the skin of a woman, and described the very physical changes that take place in a woman's body as it prepared to nurture life deep inside it — and the equally 'real' physical trauma when the baby was snatched from her and tossed on a rubbish heap by the roadside, possibly because it was illegitimate and therefore not likely to be accepted by respectable society. And again in *Shahdole ka Chooha* ('The Rat of Shahdole') Manto talked of a mother's despair in giving up her son as *mannat* at a saint's shrine where a perfectly healthy baby was 'miraculously' disfigured and mutilated into a rat-boy before being sold to an itinerant *tamashawala*. A scathing attack on the shrines that thrive on poor, desperate and superstitious people, the story derived its punch from a mother's steadfast desire to keep her son's memory alive inside her heart.

Similarly, *Khuda ki Qasam* was a mother's refusal to accept that her daughter may have been killed in the communal riots that heralded the partition of the sub-continent. Old, blind and nearly half-crazed with grief, she cannot believe anyone can kill a girl as beautiful as her daughter. In the end, she finds peace in death when she spots her daughter unexpectedly on the street one day, married though she is to the man who had abducted her. A most unexpected story was *Dhandas* (Comfort). A young widow is raped at a family wedding. Initially angry and inconsolable, she finds comfort in the arms of another man, one who offers comfort, immediately thereafter!

In *Bismillah* a woman by the strange, eponymous name, was the object of a man's lust, though she appeared to be the legally wedded wife of another man. Saeed is attracted, in equal measure, by Bismillah's large, sad-looking eyes as well as the lush fullness of her breasts and torn between voyeuristic delight in a woman's body and the prick of his own conscience. In the end, it turns out that the sullen, sphinx-like young woman is not his friend Zaheer's wife; she is a Hindu girl who got left behind during the riots and is being forced into prostitution

Introduction

by Zaheer who had been, all along, posing as a loving husband and budding film-maker.

Many who do not see Manto's prolific outpouring over a period of 20-odd years, often regard him as a writer unhealthily obsessed with sex and, by extension, women. It is important to see stories like *Thanda Gosht, Khol Do, Kaali Shalwar, Boo, Hatak* or any of the other prostitute related stories in their context and also their place in Manto's oeuvre. While it is true that Manto's prostitute is a far cry from Mirza Ruswa's Umrao Jaan or Qazi Abdul Ghaffar's Laila who were victims, creatures more sinned against than sinning, Manto's women like Sugandhi, Sultana and countless unnamed others seem willing participants in the trade of their bodies.

Women occupied a central position in a great deal of Rajinder Singh Bedi's writings too and he has etched some memorable female characters: the eponymous Kalyani and Lajwanti, Indu in *Apne Dukh Mujhe De Do* ('Give Me Your Sorrows'), Rano in *Ek Chaadar Maili Si* ('A Slightly Soiled Sheet') and Ma in *Banj* ('Barren Woman'). Details of everyday life, no matter how small, found a place in his stories and became reflections of a larger social reality. Bedi's stories survive the test of time because they hinge on the common and the commonplace that transcends time and circumstance. Human desires and aspiration just as much as human foibles and frailties neither change nor date; they are ageless and eternal — in men and women.

Ismat wrote bold stories that challenged traditional morality and worn-out notions of a woman's 'place' in society. Given her interest in sexual matters, comparisons between her and Manto have always been inevitable. Like Manto's *Boo* she faced terrible flak for her story, *Lihaaf*, published in *Adab-e-Latif* in 1942. While her interest was primarily in women, it is also true that she saw women in the larger social context. She

11

wrote stories (*Jadein*) and plays (*Dhaani Bankein*) on communal tensions, issues that did not concern women alone but issues that can be viewed from a unique perspective because they come from a woman's pen. She used wit and satire as tools to sharpen her depiction of social realities and give an extra edge to her pithy, flavoursome, idiomatic language, the *begumaati zuban* that she herself knew so well. In her hands, Urdu acquired a new zest, an added spice that made it not only more readable but also better equipped to reflect new concerns, concerns that had been hitherto considered beyond the pale of literature.

While Ismat was the tallest among the women writers of her generation, those who also made their mark were Hajira Masrur, Khadija Mastur, Siddiqa Begum Seoharvi, Shakila Akhtar, and Sarla Devi. None of these women, however, matched the vim and vigour of Rashid Jahan or Ismat Chughtai. Dr Rashid Jahan was Ismat's predecessor and she can be credited with, in a sense, 'showing the way' to writers such as Ismat. Rashid Jahan's desire to write stories primarily about women can be traced to her father's decision to start a school for girls in Aligarh (the present-day Women's College): in both we see an inherent desire for education and uplift. In the father's case through a pioneering attempt to provide modern, scientific education to girls in a safe and secure environment; in the daughter's case through a more radical, more explicitly anti-colonial, more reformist desire to 'expose' and thereby bring about change in the status of women. Muslim social reformers — be it Rokeya Sekhawat Hossein in Bengal, Maulvi Karamat Husain in Lucknow and to a certain extent the enlightened Begums of Bhopal — had all along concentrated on the education of the girl child. No one, till Rashid Jahan burst upon the scene, had spoken so openly about other matters that concerned women just as much as their education, namely, their reproductive

Introduction

health, sexually transmitted diseases, oppressive marriages, the inequality between the sexes, etc.

Rashid Jahan explored the relationship between men and women both from the lower sections of society as well as the educated middle class. In an unusual story that comprised entirely of a dialogue between an unnamed man and woman, *Mard wa Aurat* (Man and Woman), a man proposes to a woman but instead of a happily-ever-after ending they come upon the stumbling block of her job which she refuses to abandon for the sake of matrimony. The man makes snide references to her job which only fetches a measly Rs 100, to which the woman says: 'Whatever it may be; it is the key to my freedom' and 'freedom implies standing on one's own feet.' From the question of job and salary, the disagreement goes on to other issues that plague all marriages: who to meet who not to meet, who one likes and who one doesn't, to sit at home and 'look after the house' or go out and have a life; the dialogue ends with the man asserting his natural superiority over the woman. A short, short story, like many others written by Rashid Jahan, it presents age-old questions about men and women making the story at once ageless and universal. A lighter, humorous take on marriage is found in *Gosha-e-Aafiyat*, where a group of husbands form a club or band to escape nagging quarrelsome wives! It is also a spoof at the vacuous, club-going newly-westernised Indians who were freshly introduced to the delights of dancing openly with the wives of other men and greater social interaction between the sexes.

Other women-centric writing came from writers such as Upendranath Ashk's short stories in *Aurat ki Fitrat* 'Woman's Temperament', Khwaja Ahmad Abbas's collection of stories entitled *Ek Ladki* ('A Girl'), Qazi Abdul Ghaffar's *Laila ke Khutoot* ('Letters of Laila').

13

The Woman in Urdu Poetry

In Urdu poetry, the beloved has always been a bit of a mystery wrapped in an enigma. While the voice may be that of a lovelorn woman suffering from the pangs of separation, a discontented concubine, or a young woman on the verge of marriage, the object of these passionate outpourings of both requited and unrequited love could just as well be man, woman or child!

Since Urdu poetry has largely been a male preserve and there has been only a sprinkling of women poets, that too in recent times, men have produced the bulk of Urdu poetry. And it has been regarded as perfectly acceptable for men to write in women's voices on so-called women's issues expressing womanly concerns. This vocal masquerade has been taking place for centuries and has been taken rather quite for granted.

Vast amounts of Urdu poetry have been written by men but narrated in the feminine voice to express both erotic and spiritual love. Incidentally, love in Urdu poetry can be *ishq-e-majazi* or 'symbolic' love or *ishq-e-haqiqi* or 'real' love; disconcerting for the uninitiated is the realisation that the former is earthly, carnal or erotic and the latter is spiritual, sublime, mystical.

Given below is a sampling of the different voices and concerns in Urdu poetry regarding women: ranging from idealisation to deification to empathy:

> *Abhi raushan hua jaata hai rasta*
> *Woh dekho aurat aa rahi hai*
>
> —Shakeel Jamali
>
> The road is about to be illuminated
> Look, a woman is coming this way

Introduction

Chalti phirti hui aankhon se azaan dekhi hai
Main ne jannat to nahin dekhi hai maa dekhi hai
                                        —Munawwar Rana
With my own eyes I have seen the call to prayer
I have not seen heaven but I have seen a mother

Aurat ne janam diya mardon ko mardon ne use bazaar diya
Jab ji chaha masla kuchla jab ji chaha dhutkar diya
                                        —Sahir Ludhianvi
Woman gave birth to man, men gave her the marketplace
When it suited them they crushed her or scolded her

Occasionally, there would be a voice such as Majaz who showed women another way of seeing their own lot:

Tere mathe pe yeh aanchal to bahut hii khuub hai lekin
Tu iss aanchal se ik parcham bana leti to achchha tha

The veil on your forehead is very pretty indeed
It'd be better still had you fashioned a flag out of it

And here's an early take on modernity, again from Majaz:

Bataoon kya tujhe ai ham-nashin kis se mohabbat hai
Main jis duniya mein rahta huun woh iss duniya ki aurat hai

What shall I tell you my friend of her whom I love
She is a woman of the world I live in

I wanted to pick this thread, of men seeing women as inhabitants of the same world that they live in. With this intention, I set out in search of stories for this collection.

The Stories in This Selection

My task was made easy by two progressives — Rajinder Singh Bedi and Krishan Chandar — who continued to be active long after the progressive writers' movement had petered off. Nurtured by a literary movement and a body of writers that prided in looking at women as comrades-in-arms, both have written powerful female characters but both can be occasionally guilty of a sentimentalism, a tendency to idealise a woman in an attempt to appear even-handed. The first story in this collection, 'Woman' (*Aurat*) by Bedi shows the writer struggling to shake off a centuries-old conditioning, one that sees a woman as a nurturer, a preserver of a life force no matter how flawed or frugal that life force might be. A father might be willing to get rid of a child that is less-than-perfect, a bit like a vet that puts diseased or broken animals to sleep, but a mother can never envisage such an idea. Added to this view is the familiar trope of unrequited love, that too for a damsel in distress, of a male viewer drawn to a woman who loves her child unconditionally. This ability to love makes everything about her so attractive: 'I don't know if she was beautiful in real life but in my fantasy she was extremely attractive. I really liked the way she patted her hair in place. She would flick her hair off her face, stroke them in place with her fingers, stretching her hands all the way behind her shoulders — making it so difficult for me to decide if this was a conscious habit or an involuntary action.'

Krishan Chandar's 'Preeto', also the title story for this collection, has two seemingly unrelated tracks that converge in a most unexpected manner: both lead to a point where the woman is eventually perceived

Introduction

as beautiful and enigmatic, the depths of whose heart can never be plumbed by a man. While one track leads to a gruesome tragedy, the other leads nowhere. The parallel tracks meet at a point of sorrowful acknowledgement: 'A woman never forgets. Those people do not know women who think she comes to your home in a palanquin, sleeps on your bed, gives you four children and in return you can snatch her dream away, such people don't know women. A woman never forgets.' A man may love her and pamper her but there is no knowing that she will love him in return or that she will ever fully reveal what lies buried beneath seeming normalcy.

Gulzar heralds the onset of modernity in Urdu literature. In his story, a woman may work and play the field, she may find love outside marriage, she may stray as far as her former husband but she is still tethered to the yoke of motherhood, of being answerable to a man: in this case her son, a 13-year old boy who stops being her son the moment he turns a male gaze at her. The same son who is willing to stand up for her when she is a woman wronged, a victim, turns against her when she is perceived as a woman who has committed a wrong and set foot outside the proverbial *lakshman rekha* or line of chastity and honour. Gulzar's 'Man' ('*Mard*') reminds us how ingrained these notions of honour are and how stringently women, more than men, must subscribe to them.

Faiyyaz Rifat's 'Shonali' and Ratan Singh's 'Wedding Night' ('*Suhaag Raat*') are classic instances of the male gaze: one is directed by an older man at a young nubile servant and the other at a *maalan* (a girl who tends a garden). In this thinly-disguised moral tale, the flowers are symbols of 'pure' love that a girl gives her groom on her wedding night. Both stories show a preoccupation with beauty and youth, a preoccupation that is also found in Baig Ehsas's 'A Heavy Stone' '*Sang-e Giran*' and Syed Muhammad Ashraf's 'Awaiting the Zephyr' ('*Baad-e Saba ka Intizar*'). Deepak Budki's

'Driftwood' and Hussainul Haque's 'The Unexpected Disaster' (*'Naagahaanii'*) are troubling stories: the former makes a case for women who have been victims of abuse in childhood (incest in this case) becoming wayward and wilful as adults and the latter for victims of marital abuse having every reason to find love outside a loveless marriage yet refraining from doing so out of a sense of honour and uprightness. Both stories, in a sense, dwell on the notion of moral turpitude and its opposite, a dignity that men expect from women.

Zamiruddin Ahmad's 'A Bit Odd' (*'Kuchh Ajeeb Sa'*) is a niggling look at the idea of dignity, a quality that is intrinsic to women in a patriarchal world view and is only enhanced by the institutions of marriage, home, religion, domesticity. Abdus Samad probes a woman's heart, scouring the ashes for a lambent flame in 'Ash in the Fire' (*'Aag Mein Raakh'*): a thick blanket may douse a fire but beneath the ashes something will continue to smoulder. Rahman Abbas presents us with a contrarian view: What if a woman is self-avowedly asexual? What if she is willing to be a man's friend and companion but nothing else? Will the male gaze continue to peer and prod looking for something that does not exist? What if a woman says 'I don't feel any need. I'm a dry river'? The woman in Siddique Alam's 'The Serpent's Well' (titled *'Bain'* meaning 'lamentation' in the original but given this title by the translator) is as ancient as the forested heartland of India, and just as darkly mysterious.

To conclude, let me rest my case with these words by Milan Kundera in *The Book of Laughter and Forgetting*:

'The male glance has often been described. It is commonly said to rest coldly on a woman, measuring, weighing, evaluating, selecting her — in other words, turning her into an object... What is less commonly known is that a woman is not completely

Introduction

defenseless against that glance. If it turns her into an object, then she looks back at the man with the eyes of an object. It is though a hammer had suddenly grown eyes and stare up at the worker pounding a nail with it. When the worker sees the evil eye of the hammer, he loses his self-assurance and slams it on his thumb. The worker may be the hammer's master, but the hammer still prevails. A tool knows exactly how it is meant to be handled, while the user of the tool can only have an approximate idea.'

While a woman is certainly no tool, nor should she know how to be 'handled', there is something to be said for returning the gaze, of looking back. Perhaps if more women were to turn a steady gaze back at the beholder, there is no knowing what the 'seeing eye' will see.

Rakhshanda Jalil
New Delhi

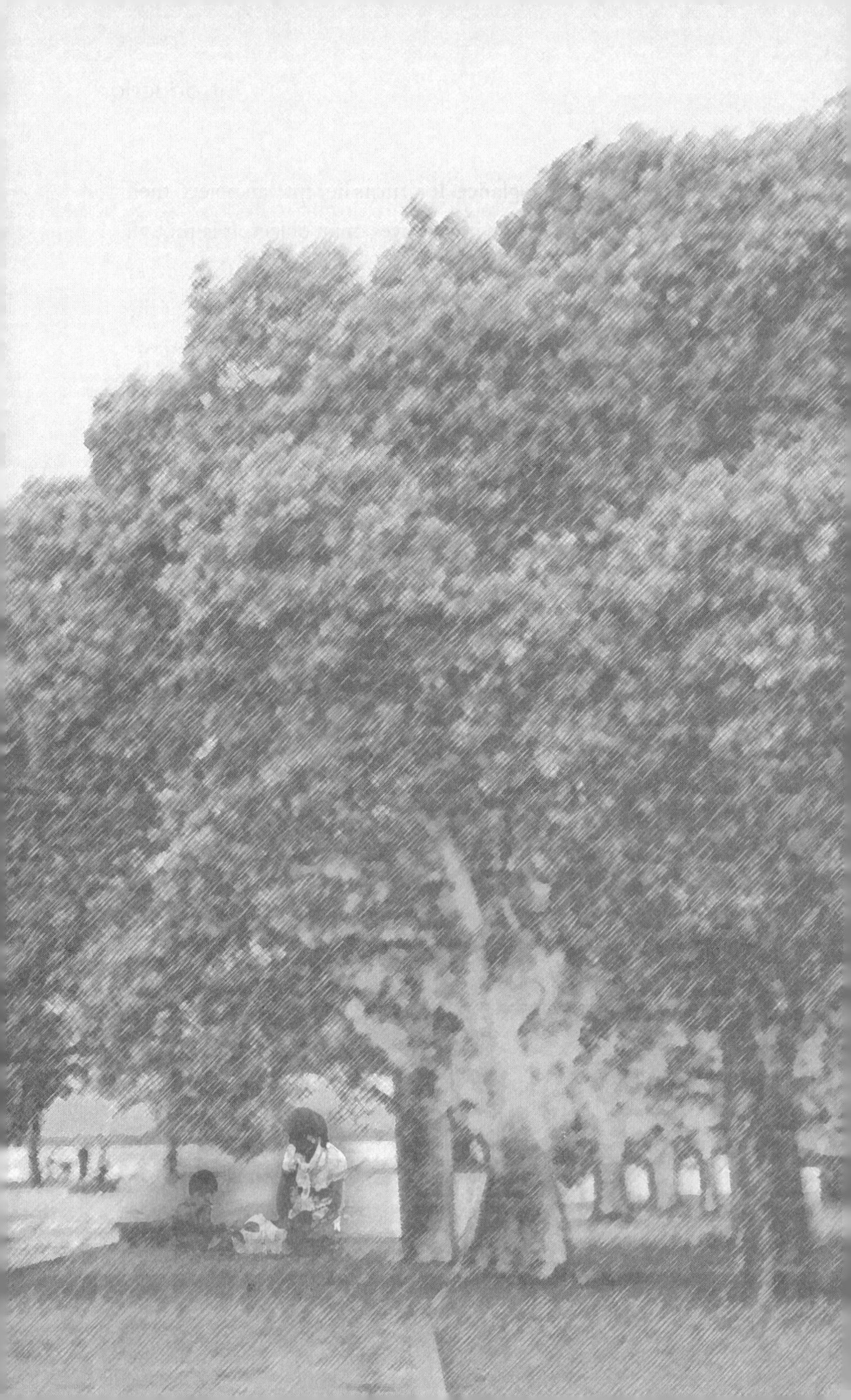

Woman

Rajinder Singh Bedi

Inside Naseem Bagh, which faced Town Hall, there were perhaps just two or maybe three things that caught my attention. A tall sumbul tree that was covered in moss. To me it seemed to be wearing a beautiful, rich green coat. It would sway unsteadily in the wind quite like an intoxicated man. Then, there was this student, whose antics caught my attention. Usually with his books scattered about quite far away from him, he liked to sing a particular song in English. The essence of that song was: 'When winter is here, can spring be far behind?'

I also noticed a young woman about twenty or twenty-one years old. She would often be seen fervently kissing the drooling face of her child who clearly suffered from some form of mental disability. She usually wore a simple white saree. It was quite evident from her demeanour that she detested people coming close to her!

Initially, when I noticed her, I felt she was perhaps hungry. But soon after I saw her buy a few tangerines and scatter them in front of her child. If she was indeed hungry she would have at least tasted one of those oranges. Then, I thought maybe her hunger is more sensual in nature. But if this were true then she would not adopt this 'stand-off, don't touch me' air about her. What is more, she would have opted for some bright colours like other women her age.

Her child appeared quite repulsive to me. Being partly paralysed, his face was always covered with saliva and drool. His mother would try to wipe his face and chin many times but in protest the child would shake his head to and fro and as soon as he was wiped clean he would make more saliva bubbles which would cover his face all over again and, in the process, appear even more unpleasant. And then he would laugh in a meaningless idiotic manner while his mother, in a burst of true happiness, would start weeping.

Later, I began to notice a black car that drew up at the gate of Naseem Bagh every day; its driver would shamelessly honk loudly as it approached her gate. A well-built man, wearing a *churidaar pajama* with its drawstring habitually showing up under his muslin *kurta*, would step out of the car. His mouth was usually stuffed with paan.

A closer look revealed his bloodshot eyes, his breath gave ample proof of him being an alcoholic. Maybe he was responsible for the paralytic state of that child! He would try to come closer to that woman, with lust in his eyes, he would try to hold her arm and try to take her towards the car. His possessive gesture indicated he could well be the husband of the woman but a father to that child?

Even as the husband called out to her, the wife would continue to play with her child almost obsessively, in an intense, near-frenzied manner. For a while, the husband would sit on a tree stump and watch his wife's fanatical behaviour. After some time, with a frigid glance thrown in his direction, she would continue to fold away the little clothes of the child and gather his plastic toys. As the sound of the car horn became louder, so did the woman's frenzy.

Woman: Rajinder singh bedi

I was beginning to feel a kind of attachment towards that woman. My increasing interest in her led me to believe there was a justification in all her actions. I don't know if she was beautiful in real life but in my fantasy she was extremely attractive. I really liked the way she patted her hair in place. She would flick her hair off her face, stroke them in place with her fingers, stretching her hands all the way behind her shoulders — making it so difficult for me to decide if this was a conscious habit or an involuntary action.

Like her husband I too disliked her child and his saliva-smeared face. However, I felt pity as well for his helpless state and this was igniting a feeling of deep love in my heart. But, what was the point of falling in love? A love that was deeply rooted in dislike was best forgotten.

For many days I kept hoping for a chance to talk to her … almost like it happens in cheap romantic movies when a girl drops something and a boy picks it and wipes it and says 'Madam, your handkerchief …'

The girl smiles … And, just like that, love blossoms!

For many days I was watching and waiting for her to drop something so I could address her.

'Madam your … your … your …' And our love story could also blossom. But that woman was very careful and she did not give me any such chance. She used to often see me moving around her but I could not hold her attention.

One fine day eventually she felt the need to buy some tangerines. At that time the child's socks, his rubber doll and a few edibles were scattered around on the lawn. A few crows were hovering around as well. It was possible if she left to buy the oranges, the crows might attack those things and perhaps also try to harm the child's shiny eyes! The child was gradually becoming aware of his surroundings and he liked the reddish-orange colour of the tangerines. The woman tried to get up a few times but then decided against it thinking about the repercussions. I wanted to seize this opportunity to talk to her but suddenly all those words I wanted to say eluded my mind and all I could say was, 'Madam ... can I help you?'

Quite obviously these words could not have had the desired effect. With great disdain, the same disdainful look she cast towards her husband, she looked at me and said, 'No ... I do not need your help.'

Alas! My love remained locked in my heart.

The woman's husband worked in a veterinary hospital. At least that is what I could conclude from his conduct. As he spent a lot of time with animals he too seemed to have acquired inhuman tendencies. He did not feel any love for his helpless son. Whenever his wife tried to give him the child to hold he would panic and retreat saying 'Hey! Hey! My clothes will get spoilt ... my ... my ...'

Then, with a glint of lust in his eyes, he would tell his wife 'Come on, dear ... he's making a lot of noise.'

The woman was named Dammo. I gathered that from the conversations I overheard between husband and wife. Dammo is such a pretty name! If you say it softly it sounds very nice. With a sweet name like Dammo it would be so nice to pacify her if she ever got angry ... maybe I was beginning to fantasise about these things.

One day I heard her husband say, 'This is what we do at our hospital.'

'So be it,' Dammo replied with hatred in her voice.

'They are not human ...'

'They are better than humans ...'

Her husband asked with flared nostrils, 'So, you feel an injured horse should not be put to rest? You think it better if his master makes him work all day and hurts him each time with his whip?'

With disgust, Dammo glanced at him and said, 'Why can't they be freed in the wilds?'

Dammo's husband started laughing absurdly, quite like his son's laughter and then said, 'No one would give him anything to eat and he will starve to death. The decision is yours — is it better to end his suffering with just one gunshot or to let him survive and suffer each day?'

Dammo was speechless! She looked at her son's face, smeared with saliva, then with a surge of deep maternal love, pulled him close to her chest. The child made incoherent noises and waved his hands and legs. With overwhelming love, Dammo continued to hug him as tears filled her eyes.

After this incident I became aware of the fellow's dangerous intentions. It would not be a difficult task for a doctor. For a few days he could spread the word about his son's illness, then eventually stifle him. The child would make a few disgusting unintelligible noises, thrash his arms and legs wildly. But the mother would know. She would never forgive or forget this crime committed by her inhuman, alcoholic husband.

The next day, as usual, after returning from the bank, I reached the shade of the sumbul tree. That familiar student was there, trying very hard to juggle two balls with his hands. His books, as always, were scattered under the shade of another tree. Dammo too was present, with her child. I could sense that the previous day's conversation with her husband was still fresh in her mind. It was obvious, to me, that with her passionate devotion to her child, she was trying to infuse life and love in him with every passing moment.

Suddenly, the child managed to crawl away from the car and come under the shade of the sumbul tree. He was trying to chew the tasteless fruit that had fallen from the sumbul. His mother saw her child crawl for the first time and looked delighted. I stepped out from the shade of the sanobar and went to the market to buy a few brightly-coloured and expensive tangerines. When I returned to Naseem Bagh, the child was still nibbling the green tasteless fruit. I took out the oranges I had bought and put them close to the boy. He started crawling towards me. He finally caught one and for the other started moving towards my hand. I saw Dammo looking towards me and finally acknowledging my presence. I could see her feelings reflected clearly on her face. I could tell she was recalling how her inhuman husband had suggested, just a day before, that they end the life of their child only because he was an obstacle in the way of their love. She was thinking perhaps a miracle could take place and her child could walk one day! Suddenly, her face was radiant with hope.

The next day I bought a few colourful balloons from the market and after tying them with a string, kept them near the little boy. As the boy crawled towards the balloons and tried to reach out to them, I pulled the string towards me. Slowly the boy started crawling towards the balloons.

Dammo came to stand next to me and said, 'Please pull the string little by little.'

I tugged at the string again and said, 'No ... he should try to move a little faster.'

She was quiet after this and went to sit at her usual place. She came towards me again but then went back. It seemed she was not able to sit still. After a while, on the pretext of changing his dress, soiled as it was with saliva by this time, she came to stand close to me.

'Madam, who knows perhaps his illness will be cured one day,' I said to her.

Dammo's face lit up with happiness upon hearing this.

This continued for a few days. Every day, upon returning from the bank, I would get something or the other for the child. One day, I picked up the child and held him in my arms for a long time. I took out the handkerchief from my pocket and even wiped his face clean. After that I kissed his cheek.

Dammo blushed as she saw this. After some hesitation she came close towards me and smiled.

At that time the sumbul tree was swaying in the wind. That non-serious student was once again inspired to sing the song he loved:

'When winter is here, can spring be far behind?'

In that instance, as the child got down from my arms and started crawling near our feet, Dammo and I both knew a miracle could not cure him.

—*Translated by Zarine Menon*

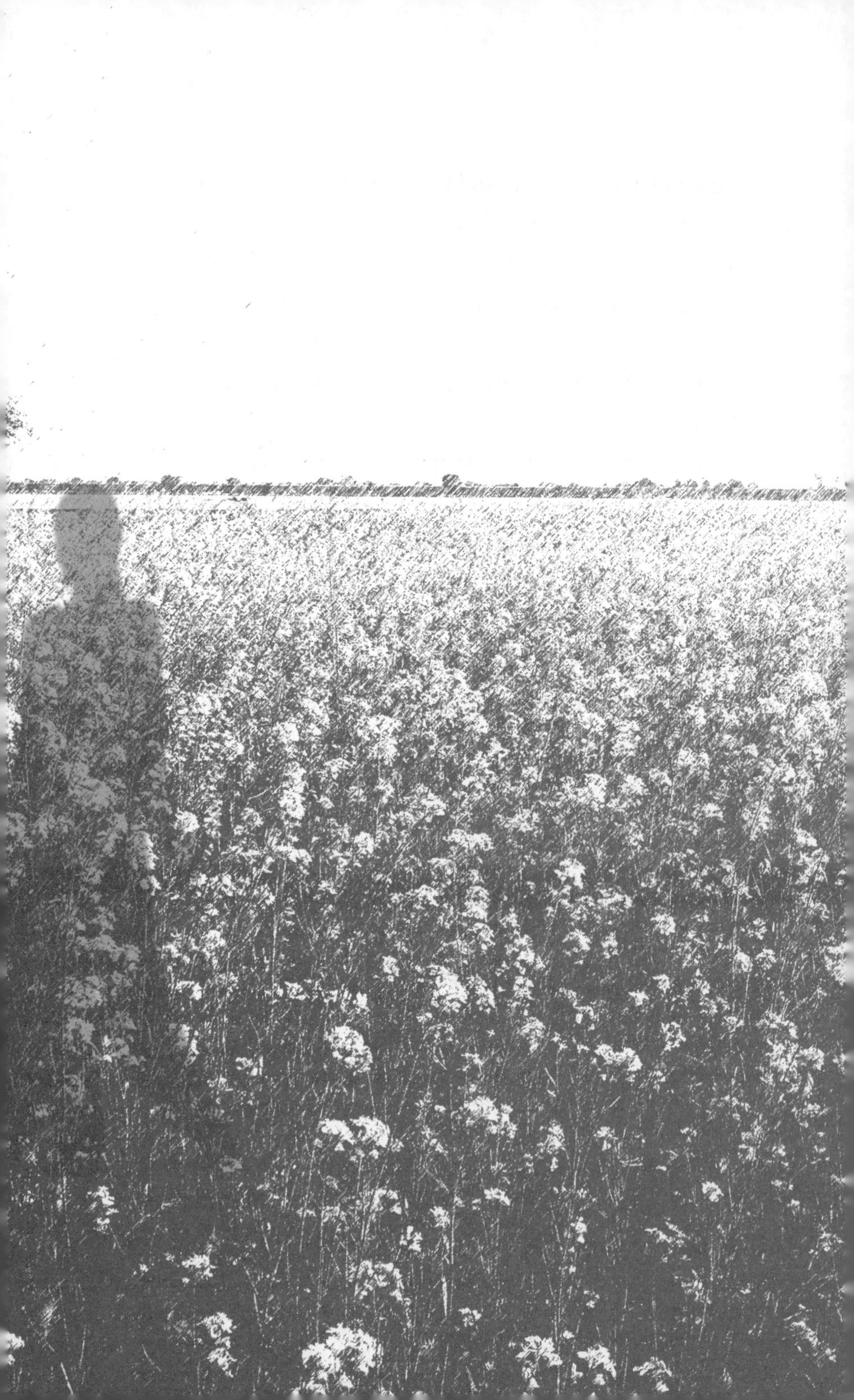

Preeto

Krishan Chandar

When he opened the door and entered the rail compartment, I could tell from the way he walked that he had worked in the army. He had an impressive personality with a body well over six feet tall, a ruddy complexion and an impressive white beard. He was dressed in a black woollen suit. In the glow of the overhead light, tiny flecks of mica in his crisply starched turban gleamed like jewels. Walking straight ahead with confident strides, he came and stood near me. He stooped to read the number on the seat next to mine and then, with a contented sigh, settled down beside me. The seat went back a little under his weight. He took another contented breath, looked at me and said, 'These reclining chairs are very good.'

I immediately put out the cigarette, which I had lit a moment ago, in the ashtray. The old Sikh looked at me and smiled, 'Thank you! I truly don't like the smoke from tobacco at all.'

I liked the look of his teeth when he smiled. They were extremely white and strong and set in perfect rows. This old Sikh 'military' man must have been no less than 70 years at least but I could see the gleam of youth and curiosity in his big black eyes. In this age too he appeared to be in extraordinary good health and there seemed to be no doubt that in his younger days he must have been an extremely good looking and handsome man. The one thing that showed most clearly on his face right now were the scars from old wounds. Three or four long scars marred both his right and left cheeks. In fact, on the right cheek the wound had made a crucifix and on the left there seemed to be a 'V' shaped scar. When he lifted his hands to straighten his tie, I noticed that there were several small scars on the back of his hands as though someone had tried to make mince meat out of his hands with a small knife.

Must have been in the war, I said to myself. It must have been in the First World War that the accident must have occurred. It was a good thing, I thought, that this good looking and virile man didn't lose an arm or a leg, or else how poorly he would have looked today.

I didn't get enough time to ponder over this as the bearer from the Restaurant Car appeared and announced: 'Please come and eat soon because we will close the restaurant at 10:00 pm.'

I got to my feet immediately. The old Sikh too got up with me.

'Even though I had eaten at 8:00 pm before leaving my house, I find I am hungry again,' the old Sikh smiled as he addressed me.

'And I am eating so late because I wasn't hungry earlier,' I answered.

The two of us went and sat down in the Dining Car. There was no one there except the bearers and a young couple sitting at a corner table. They were drinking coffee as they gazed at the full moon outside the window. The girl's hand was in the man's and, from time to time, he would press it gently; the girl's face would break into a radiant smile as though the man had pressed a switch in her hand and an electric current had coursed through her making her face light up like a bulb. The girl's hair was cut in

Preeto: Krishan Chandar

a pleasing style and she had a beautiful face and a very attractive air about her. From her features you could tell that she was a native Christian with some amount of European blood too in her. The man, however, was pure Indian: with a somewhat dark complexion, short statured but compact and strongly built with thick gleaming hair, a wide jaw line that was smooth and freshly shaved. His hair looked freshly cut and groomed; in fact, it seemed as though he had got his hair cut this very day! His clothes too were immaculate; good health and vigour oozed out of every pore of his body.

In his hand he held one hand of the girl which he would press repeatedly as though he was trying to pump an electric current into it. With the other hand he was ceaselessly crumpling the loose end of her blue sari. His small but gleaming black eyes were looking at the girl as though she was not a girl but a plateful of beauty!

'There is such a strong element of health in his romance,' I said as I patted my own somewhat sallow cheeks.

The old Sikh said nothing in response because by now our food had been placed before us and he was busy inspecting it with utmost concentration. While we were eating, the young couple finished their coffee, paid the bill and left. As the girl was leaving, she again flashed that radiant smile. I found myself liking that girl and her lovely smile very much indeed. There was such affection and belonging in the look she directed at the man. Sometimes a woman gives everything away in one glance and stands by looking like an empty vessel, alone and innocent. And at that moment she also looks her loveliest.

The girl had smiled and then looked at her companion in just such a manner. While she held his hand, he put his other arm around her waist and guided her towards the vestibule outside the dining car. The restaurant began to look even more desolate after they had gone. It seemed to me as though the moon hanging in the window had been strung there just for those two. I reached out and drew the curtain.

The old Sikh smiled at my action but continued to eat quietly. After he had finished eating, he ordered coffee whereas I stepped out into the vestibule to smoke a cigarette. In one corner, the young man was kissing the girl. Moonlight was streaming on to her face and I could see the tears flowing from her eyes.

The man looked at her in surprise and asked, 'Why the tears?'

'Nothing, just like that,' the girl wiped her eyes as she answered. Then she broke out into a tinkling laugh and, once again, her face was lit by that radiant smile, the smile that tugged at one's heart strings.

The man kissed her once again.

The girl's shoulders trembled. She said, 'Come, darling, let's go inside; it's cold here.' With her eyes, she silently made a sign towards me as I stood on one side ostensibly looking out of the window at the full moon outside. The man looked at me as though he would stab me with a dagger there and then. But he slowly turned around and, putting his arm around the girl, took her out of the vestibule and into the compartment.

After some time, a guard come into our compartment and put out all the lights. But the moon was full and bright outside and in its white, gentle light the faces of the sleeping silent passengers were clearly visible.

'I can't sleep in this moonlight; is it all right if I draw the curtain?' I asked my fellow passenger.

'Just wait a while,' the old Sikh answered in a low intense voice. 'This full moon night is terrifying, terrifying and beautiful! I am scared of it but I also want to see it. Can I see this moon for just a little while longer?'

'Young people watch the moon; it isn't something that people your age and mine are supposed to do,' I answered with a sad smile.

The old Sikh too smiled. His right cheek was in the full glare of the moonlight and the sign of the cross looked deeply gouged in it. The 'V' on the left cheek was lost in the darkness.

'Did you get these scars on your face in the war?' I asked him.

'War?' the old Sikh looked at me. And looking as though he was getting lost somewhere deep inside himself he answered softly, 'Yes it was a war after all.'

'Which war? The First World War? Or some other war before that?'

'I was never in the Army,' the old Sikh answered softly.

My curiosity was whetted by the fact that my assumption had turned out to be wrong about him. So I asked him, 'How did you get these wounds, then?'

The old Sikh looked this way and that. The moon was in its place. So was the window. There was a smattering of passengers in the compartment but they were all in their places, fast asleep in the comfortable reclining chairs. About five or six rows ahead of us, in the dark corner in the first row, the man and the girl were crouched in their seats. The girl's head was resting on the man's shoulder and his arm was looped around her shoulder. Both seemed to have their eyes shut.

The old Sikh asked me, 'Do you really want to know about it?'

'Yes, please tell me if you are not too sleepy.'

'I will never be able to sleep in this moonlight,' he answered in a mild, affable tone. And then he began to speak as though he had decided to tell a story. He drew a long deep breath and said, 'All right then, so listen! You are a complete stranger so there is no harm in telling you.'

The train window had double glazing so the loud clank of the chugging wheels was reaching my ears like a low, sweet, resonant hum. And outside, in the white light of the moon, the dark trees looked like criminals with their branches gathered close to their bosom and their heads bent low.

With a gesture towards the young man asleep in the far corner, the Sikh said, 'In my youth I too was carefree and arrogant. My father, Gajinder Singh, was the *numberdar* of Muza Hasla and apart from that Chak No. 37 was entirely under our control. There was no shortage of anything in our house. My father had got me to do a BA but I was always interested in working in the fields since a very young age. My hands were better engaged in wielding a plough than a pen. I don't know how I managed to finish my BA. My father's great desire was that I should join the Army and become a Colonel but I liked life in the fields. The moist scent of brown earth, the green pods of tender peas drenched in dew, rows of women going to fetch water from a stream, and my fast-paced golden mare trotting along and licking little clouds of dust ... Aah!'

I said, 'You must have been a very handsome man in your younger days. Women must have been besotted with you.'

The old Sikh answered with a faint smile, 'I can't remember that anyone had ever loved me so. Though, yes, once I was madly in love with a girl.'

Preeto: Krishan Chandar

'Who was she?'

'My wife.'

'Wife?'

'When I finished my BA and came home, my father got me married to Preeto, the daughter of the *numberdar* of Chak Jhamru. Preeto was a beautiful girl. Tall, slim, fair and golden, nimble and soft but I was mad over her eyes.'

'Why? What was so special about her eyes?'

'There was nothing out of the ordinary, actually; they were big and black.'

'But a lot of women have such eyes! What was so remarkable about hers?'

'I can't say. It was the colour of those eyes ... No, no, not the colour ... it was the tone and tenor of those eyes that made them so different.'

'Those eyes spoke?'

'They didn't actually speak but I think they wanted to. It seemed as though they would say something, but they never did say anything to me. All the time, they seemed to be just dreaming. Have you ever seen eyes that seem to be dreaming all the time?'

'All eyes dream in their youth,' I answered.

'Yes, but everyone has different dreams,' the old Sikh said softly. 'I was completely smitten by my Preeto. You might say that was because there had been no girl in my life before her, and no one after her ... But you have not seen Preeto or else you would not say that. She was the sort of girl you could love madly even though she was your wife. When I returned home and chose to work in my fields rather than join the Army, my father immediately got me married off. He set me to work in the fields even though he must have been very disappointed. However, I was perfectly happy. Had I been in the Army, how would I have loved my Preeto? By now I would have been dead in some war or the other of the *firangis* in Italy or France or Mesopotamia ... though I cannot say whether what eventually happened was better, or worse.'

And suddenly he fell silent.

I too remained quiet.

After a long time, he said, 'To cut a long story short, I was madly in love with my Preeto and she too loved me. Not for a day were we separated from each other. But six months into our marriage, my father-in-law fell ill and Preeto had to go to her parent's home. After all, her father was ill so how could I stop her? Preeto went away and nothing interested me anymore — not my home or my fields or even my horse riding. Somehow or the other, I managed to get through three days but on the fourth day I saddled my mare and dashed off towards my in-laws' place. Chak Jhamru is at a distance of 30 *kos* from our home. But my mare was swift footed and I reached there by the time evening fell. Upon reaching Chak Jhamru I found that my father-in-law's condition had vastly improved; if anything, I found him perfectly hale and hearty. Both my father and mother-in-law were extremely pleased to see me and when they found out that the son-in-law had dropped in to enquire about his father-in-law's health, they were very pleased by my good manners. I was tired after travelling all day and so, soon after eating my dinner, I went off to sleep. I knew that I would only wake up the next morning. I told Preeto to wake me up early the next morning for I planned to go riding. I didn't want to sleep till the sun had come up.

'But it so happened that I woke up at some point in the third watch of the night. I was surprised to see that my wife was not in the bed with me. At the far end of the room, I heard the sound of the door closing softly and saw a dark shadow slipping out of the door. I rubbed my eyes and sat up. By the Dear Guru, what was going on? I got out of bed quietly. Without making a sound, I picked up the *kirpan* from under my pillow, put it on, opened the door and came out of the room.

'Outside, it was a moonlit night just like tonight. The moonlight was beautiful and full of fragrances. The birds hidden in their nests among the mustard and the sheesham trees would let out the occasional chirp in their sleep but their mates would immediately nudge them with their strong beaks and lull them back to sleep. Soon, my feet were drenched in dew. All around me tender green mustard leaves were swaying in the breeze. And I was following my Preeto through the fields.

'At first I thought she was going into the fields to answer the call of nature but when she passed the first field, then the second and climbing down the ditch that ran along the boundary of the third field, crossed the dry stream bed and disappeared from sight that I began to experience a strange anxiety, surprise and frustration. I felt as though I had been punched in my heart. But I decided to follow her with extreme caution and without making a sound so that she wouldn't know that someone was following her. I too got off the ditch that skirted the third field, crossed the dry stream bed and, with the utmost caution, peered from behind a mound.

'There were more mustard fields in front of me and a well in the middle of one of the fields. Beside the well, in the shade of a large patch of wild berries a cot had been laid out. A short distance from the cot stood a mud hut whose door was partly ajar.

'And my wife was lying on that bed with a Jat. My Preeto, my goddess, was making mad, passionate love with him. She was kissing his eyes and his cheeks repeatedly and passionately. I could feel my blood boil but I kept standing silently behind the berry patch and watched them making love. Yes, yes ... I saw everything with my own eyes.

'After some time, the Jat said to my wife: "Preeto, I am thirsty; get me some water from inside."

'Preeto raised her head from his shoulder and said: "Bachne, hasn't your thirst been slaked yet?" Bachna simply smiled in response and kissed my wife on her lips. Preeto got off the bed and went inside the mud hut through the partly ajar door. Bachna lay on his stomach and looked towards the door with great anticipation because my wife was completely naked.

'Suddenly, I took out my *kirpan* and, holding it with both my hands, raised my head and slashed Bachna with all my might. A muffled sound emerged from Bachna's lips.

'In the very next instant, Bachna's neck was severed and I dashed back to the patch of berries and disappeared in the fields. Then I retraced my steps to the mound and crossed the dry stream bed and the mustard fields. For a few seconds I stopped to wipe my *kirpan* and clean it thoroughly with loose earth and, when it became clean and gleamed like a mirror, I put it back in its sheath and entered the house. I went back to my room and lay down on the bed.

'About 30-45 minutes later Preeto entered the room very softly. I was awake but I kept my eyes closed and began to draw deep, steady breaths. Preeto opened the door and first peered closely at me. Then, very carefully, she pulled out the *kirpan* from under my pillow, unsheathed it and inspected it closely. But when she found it spotlessly clean the suspicion in her heart melted away and she lay down on the bed beside me. Silently, still as a stone!'

The old Sikh fell silent.

After a few moments of anxious waiting, I asked, with great curiosity, 'And then what happened?'

'Nothing happened. Since her father had recovered, I took Preeto and returned to our village the very next day and we continued to live together happily.

'Days passed, then months and years. I never mentioned that incident. Nor did Preeto ever let it show that she suspected something, or that she was grieving over anything. Though, yes, I did notice one thing: she never went back to her parents' home ever again. Even when I asked her to go or when her father urged her to visit, she never ever did. So much so that, with time, even I forgot all about that incident especially now that I had children. Mine and Preeto's children: two boys and a girl. Such beautiful children they were! Our Partap, Daleep and Harnam Kaur ... with time they too grew up and began to go to school and then to college. By the time they started college, our third son was born: Harbans Singh. There was great contentment and happiness in our home. Comfort and peace, trust and companionship — all the hallmarks of an exemplary family life.

'One evening, I had returned from the fields and was sitting under the *mukh*. Partap and Daleep were back from the college for the summer vacations. Harnam was sitting in her corner with her embroidery. My seven-year old Harbans was trying to ride his wooden horse. Preeto was making corn roti on the open fire under the *mukh*. Mustard leaves were boiling in another pot on the fire and its earthy scent was whetting my appetite even more. I untied my *kirpan* and kept it to one side. Then, washing my hands and face, sat down on a low stool in front of Preeto. And like a child, I began to demand food.

'Preeto, give me food quickly!'

'Preeto served me first, then Partap, then Daleep, and then Harnam Kaur. The youngest, Harbans, said, "I will eat with mother!"'

'I said to Preeto, "Why don't you also sit down now?"'

'"If I were to sit down, who would feed you?" Preeto wrinkled her nose at me.

'Her cheeks were red in the light from the fire and a lock of tangled hair hung over her forehead. She looked very dear to me at that moment.

'"Ma, give me some more of the mustard greens," Daleep said as he pushed his *thaali* forward.

'I said, "If I could get some pickle from somewhere right now my pleasure in this food would be doubled."

'"The pickle is in the pantry inside," Preeto answered somewhat hesitantly.

'"So what if it is inside? Go and get it."

'Looking somewhat abashed, Preeto said, "How can I go alone? It's very dark inside. I am scared."

'"Scared?" and the words came out of my mouth unbidden. "You are scared of going into that room in front of everyone but that night when you had crossed the fields all alone you were not scared." I spoke curtly. I don't know how I said something I hadn't said for all these years. I don't know why, after all this while, these words sprang to my lips like a taunt.

Preeto: Krishan Chandar

'Preeto simply looked at me for a moment from where she sat on the floor. And in the very next moment it seemed to me as though she was standing above my head with a *kirpan* in her hand. And as a flash of lightning coursed through me I raised my hands to save myself.

'Once, twice, thrice, the *kirpan* ripped through my cheeks. To save myself I tried to stop her with my hands. I screamed: "Preeto! Preeto, stop it!" But Preeto kept attacking me like a hungry lioness till finally, in anger, I snatched the *kirpan* from her with a sudden jolt and holding it with both my hands struck her with all the strength in my body and spirit. Preeto's head was severed. It fell near Harbans's wooden horse and rolled a short distance away where my *thaali* was upturned. Her black hair came untied and lay spread out in front of me.'

The old Sikh fell silent.

I too remained quiet. The moon was suspended silently in the window like a terrifying ghost. The faces of the passengers looked pale and lifeless as though they were not human faces but masks adorned by actors in a play. Whizzing through the fields the train was moving towards some unknown destination. And the moon was strung there — helpless and ineffectual, unarmed and alone.

After a long silence, the old Sikh spoke in a sorrowful tone. 'A woman never forgets. Those people do not know women who think she comes to your home in a palanquin, sleeps on your bed, gives you four children and in return you can snatch her dream away, such people don't know women. A woman never forgets.'

The old Sikh fell silent. He passed his hand gently over the crucifix on his cheek and remained quiet. I felt as though that crucifix was embedded deep in his heart.

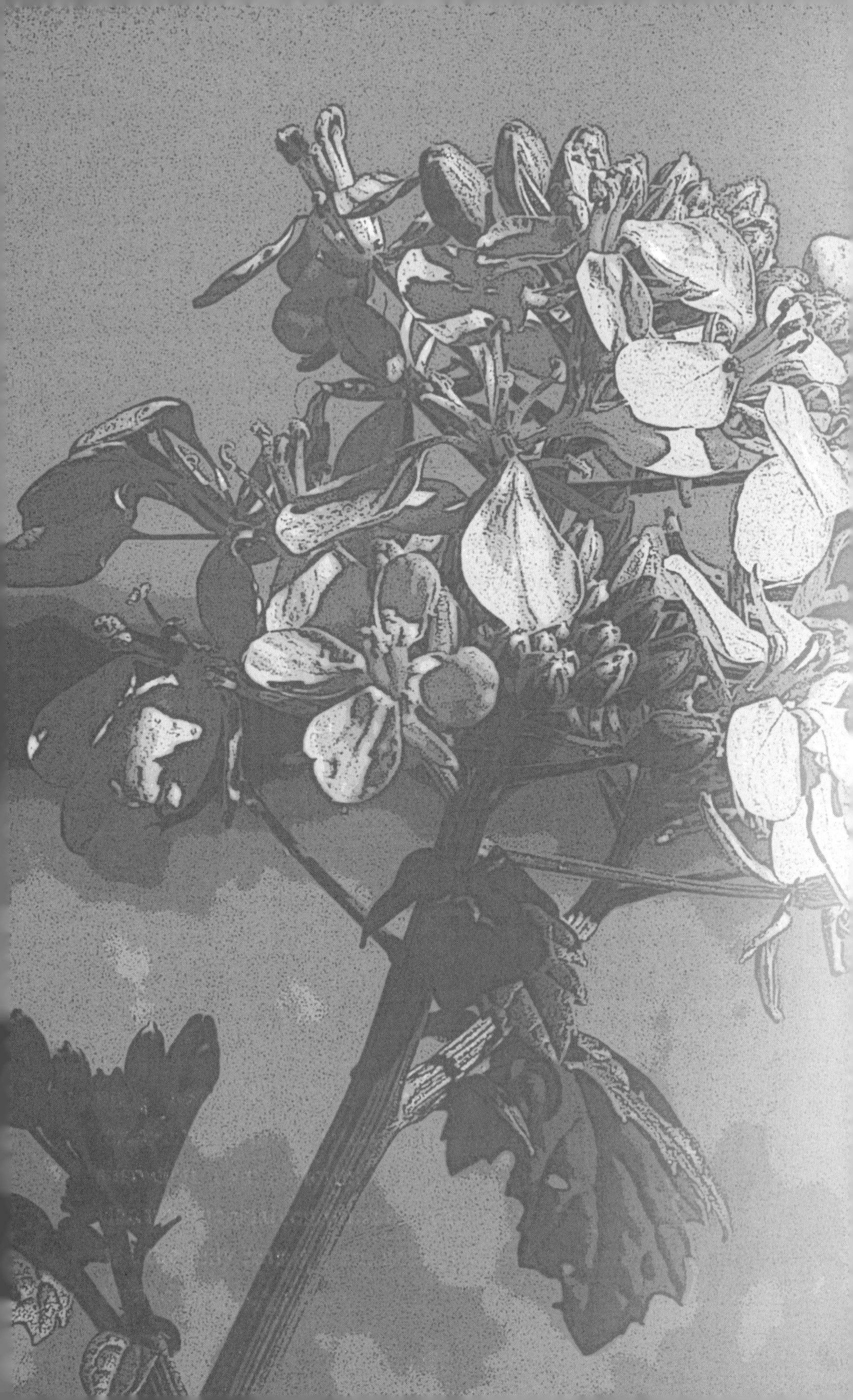

Preeto: Krishan Chandar

There was such a heavy silence in the compartment that I felt I would suffocate. I opened my mouth and took a couple of deep breaths. Suddenly my eyes fell on the young couple in the corner. The girl's hand was still in the man's and her head still rested on his shoulder. Both had their eyes closed and they seemed to be sleeping. All of a sudden, the girl raised her head from the man's shoulder. Gently she prised her fingers loose from the man's hand and looked at his face. When she was satisfied that the man was fast asleep, she removed his arm from her shoulders. She turned her face away to look at the moon and she looked at it with such longing that it contained an accusation, almost a derision, of every radiant smile that she had flashed. I was completely thrown by that look. Suddenly a *kirpan* flashed in my mind and, scared, I lowered my gaze.

In the next instant, when I raised my eyes, I saw that the girl had drawn the curtain on her window. Her face was in darkness. Even though I could not see her face I knew she was crying.

—*Translated by Rakhshanda Jalil*

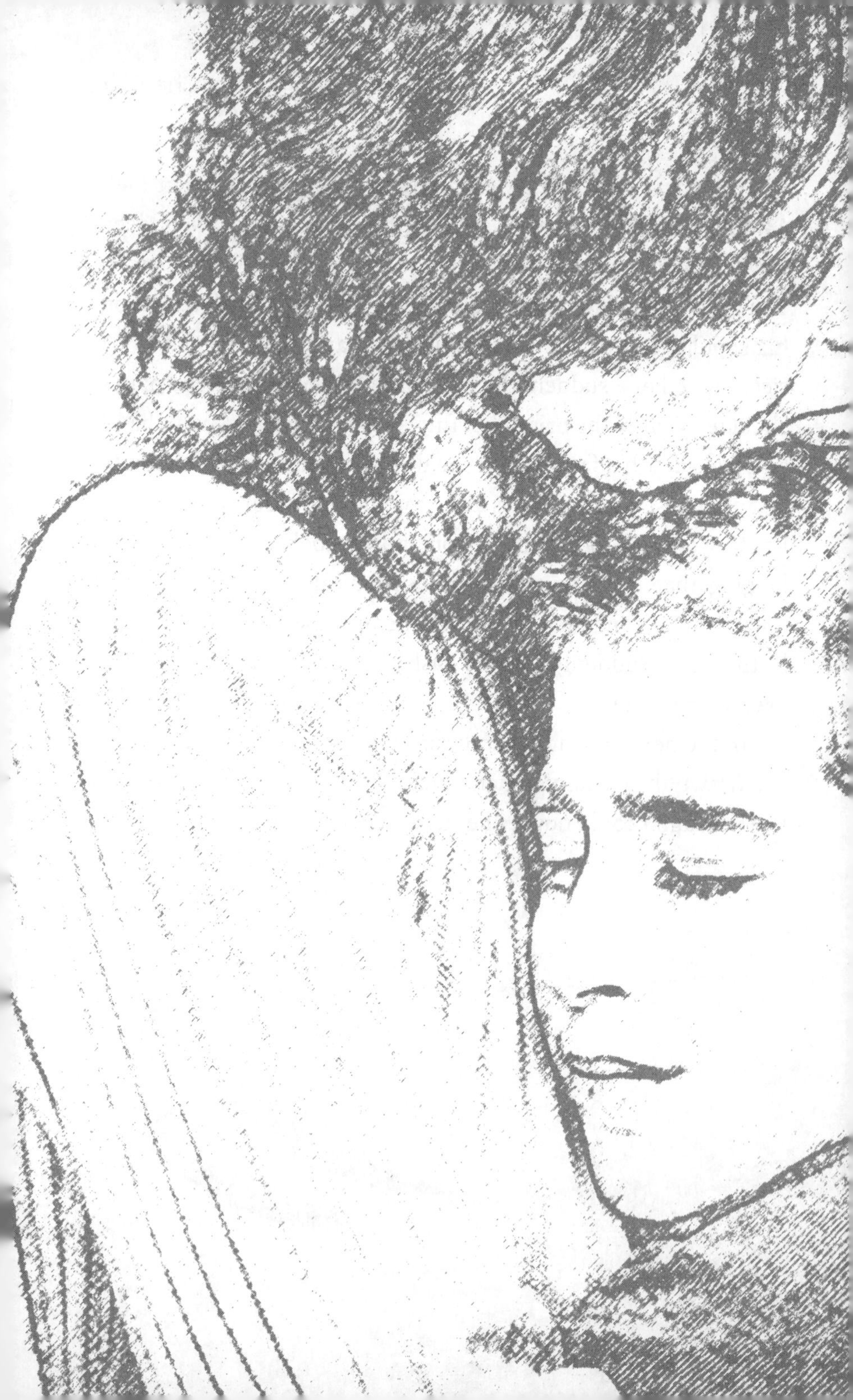

Man

Gulzar

She was worried. Her belly was beginning to show a little. Kappu was about to come home from the hostel. What if he were to ask? She was scared as though Kappu was her husband, not her son! She would have to give an explanation.

No matter what a woman might do, she always has to offer an explanation to a man. To a father, sometimes to a husband, and sometimes to a son. Bakhshi offered no explanations when he had begun to see Kanta. In fact, on the rare occasion when she did ask, the crockery would be smashed about in her house. And sometimes there would be quarrels and beatings. That is how the bitterness had increased during those days. They had both decided to put Kappu in a hostel so that he might be spared the sight of their family breaking up amidst the breaking crockery. As Bakhshi became friends with Kanta, he started losing his senses quite rapidly. Rama feared that she would not be able to save her home. And that is exactly what happened. For the telephone would ring and stop at the very first ring and then Bakhshi to call ... For Bakhshi to have office work at the oddest of times.... These were the signs. Instinctively, she knew what was going on. She could understand ...

Bakhshi began to stay away from home. Office tours were a mere excuse. She knew exactly when, where he was, and in which hotel.

Within a year she went back to work at the same bank where she used to work earlier. For this, too, she had to offer an explanation: to her father, and to Bakhshi as well. In fact, Bakhshi helped her in getting her daddy to agree. He knew it would be difficult for him to run two homes on one salary.

Her father had taken her aside and asked, 'Rama, do you two have some differences?'

Obediently, she had answered. 'No, no, Daddy, now that Kapil has gone away to the hostel, I have a lot of free time. Moreover something or the other keeps happening in one's married life.'

And her father didn't probe any further. All he said was, 'You must send Kapil to spend some time with us too.'

Both said, 'Yes, of course!' and came back from Kanpur.

Both had stopped asking for, or giving explanations. Now that everything was out in the open, what was there to explain? They had agreed to separate with civility. But the question of Kappu had remained. How would they tell him? How would they explain what had happened between them? After all, he was still a child — only nine years old.

Rama's bank manager, Raman Kumar, tried to intercede and make things better between them. But nothing came of it. She knew the intensity of Bakhshi's passion. He had loved her too like this, once.

One day, Raman Kumar had said to Rama, 'I can understand your tears but I am amazed when I see Bakhshi. His eyes well up with tears when he talks. He has never said a word against you. He even feels guilty. But ... he seems to be a very emotional person.'

She had always known that Bakhshi was wrong, but he was not false. There wasn't any artifice in the man.

Another year had passed as they had put in the divorce papers in the courts.

All this while they would go to meet Kappu in his hostel — sometimes together, and sometimes separately.

In the holidays, sometimes they would take him for trips outside Delhi; or he would come to stay with Rama while Bakhshi would be travelling away from Delhi on official work.

Kapil could sense that something was amiss. But all his young mind could say was, 'Papa doesn't love me like he used to, nor does he love you the way he used to!'

'Don't be silly! He is busy with his office work. That's all.' She didn't want Kappu's innocent mind to be affected.

'And then I have also started working in the bank!'

When the divorce had come through and Rama had wanted custody of their child, Bakhshi had not put up any resistance. He agreed. He knew he could never make his son see his point of view in Kanta's presence. He knew it would have a bad effect on his son. He continued going to see him at the hostel regularly but made no mention of having separated from his mother.

Kanta didn't last for too long. Rama didn't want Bakhshi to come back; nor did Bakhshi want to return to Rama. The crack that had come up between them was firmly in place. It was impossible to fill it up.

Now that Kapil was coming home for the holidays, Bakhshi had been transferred thousands of miles away in Chennai. Perhaps it hadn't even occurred to him that it wasn't possible for Rama to keep up the charade any longer. Rama had decided that she will tell Kappu everything. It will hurt him, certainly, for he was very close to his father. But she would prepare him for the truth gradually. All day long she would talk to him about his father and then at night by the time she would tell him everything, she knew, he would burst into tears. But she would comfort him. She would lull him to sleep ... 'I am here, my son .... your mother!'

Kappu came home and the moment he came before his mother he said, 'Ma, has Papa left us and gone? Is it true, Ma?'

Rama had not been able to control herself; she had burst out crying. Kappu had stepped forward and hugged his mother.

'I am here ... I am here ... your son!'

And she had been stunned. When do these kids grow up? No one comes to know!

That was two years ago. Kappu was coming back home again. He was 13 years old now. In the last holidays he had gone to Darjeeling with the boys and girls from his school, and she too had gone travelling for a few days with Raman Kumar. She had taken a break after many years. And when she had gone to meet Kappu at Holi, she had really wanted to bring up the subject of Raman Kumar. But she was scared. What if it had a bad effect on Kappu? After all, he was just a child!

She had been thinking about it all day now. 'After all, it isn't as though Kappu has grown up and become a man! He's still a child! He's only 13! Even if he notices my belly, he will just think I have become fat. How will he know what has happened?'

But this time she will certainly bring up Raman's name and, if possible, she will also mention that they have quietly registered their marriage. After all, in a few months' time she must also ask him ... whether he wants a brother or sister?

When Kappu came, she spent the entire day hiding her belly. She wore loose ill-fitting clothes. Not for minute did she allow the dupatta to slip from her body. She kept feeding him and thinking that she would broach the subject when he would lie down on the bed beside her at night when it was time for him to sleep.

Suddenly, there was the sound of breaking glass in his room. She ran towards it only to find that Kappu had wounded his hand. The glass flower-vase was lying shattered into smithereens on the floor.

'Kappu?'

She had barely stepped forward when Kappu pushed her away.

'Don't come near me!' His voice sounded choked. 'You have a baby in your tummy.'

Rama could feel her limbs going limp. Beads of perspiration broke out on her forehead.

'Whose child is it? Raman Uncle's? Bastard!'

It wasn't Kappu's voice; she could hear Bakhshi's. She felt it wasn't her son speaking; it was her man! A man!

—*Translated by Rakhshanda Jalil*

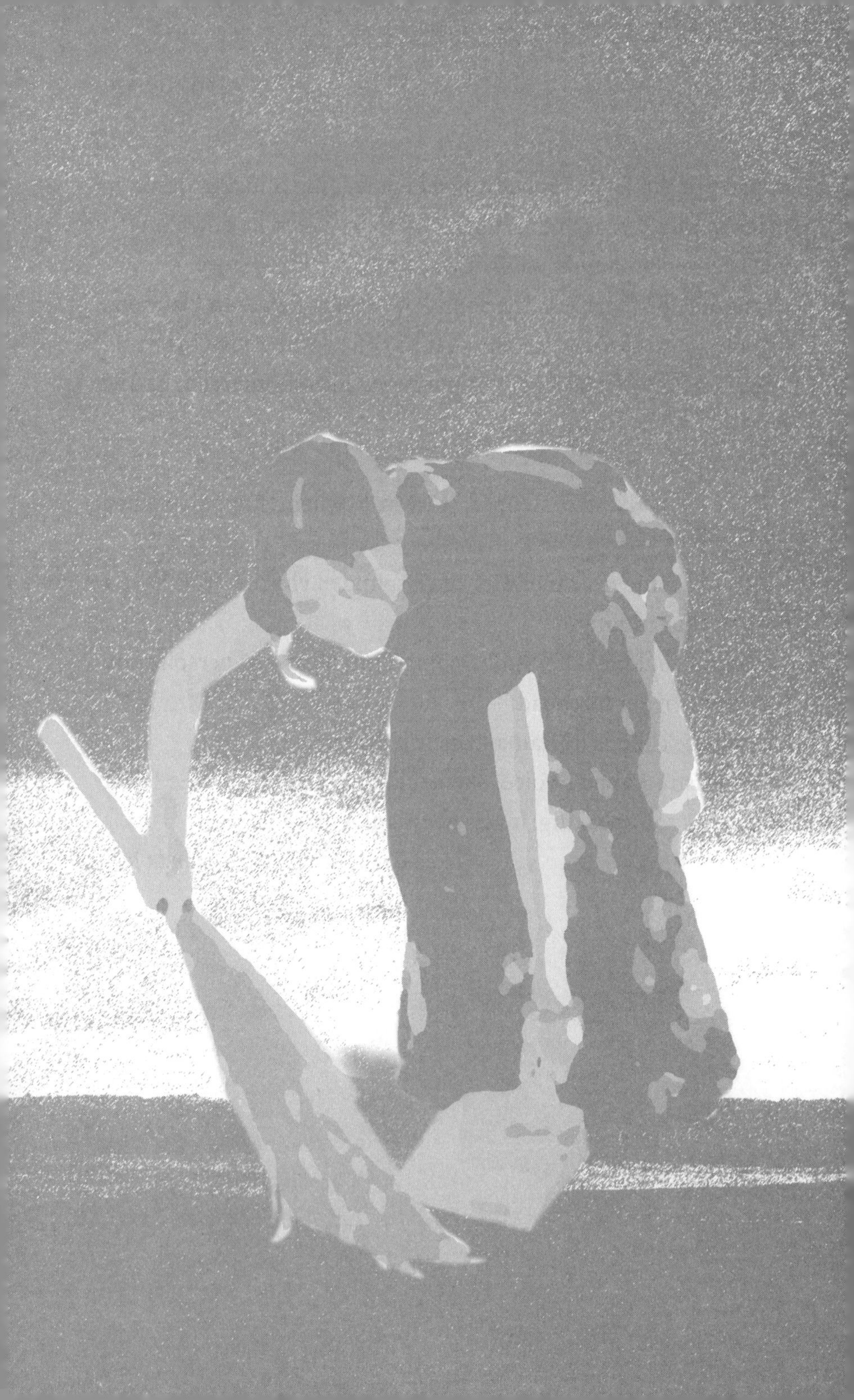

Shonali

Faiyaz Riffat

I often open my fifth-floor drawing room window and take in all the sundry faces of the passers-by below. When my eyes tire, I shut them and lose myself in the astonishing world of dreams, as human beings are wont to do. What else are these scattered broken dreams but memories mingled with a longing for the past? An ideal image, a sort of magic spell, keeps bobbing up and down in my imagination and the stresses of life become easier to bear. I've lived for years in a world of dissatisfaction and ennui. All desires and experiences are swept up in the swiftly-flowing currents of the river of time like so much detritus hell-bent upon a journey to nowhere. Mornings disappear into evenings and evenings into the dark mysteries of nights, and my sense of loss, like a demon, cuts at my being with a lancet.

That day, the first shower of rain brought freshness to my broken body. I pushed the pillow between my thighs and drank the pattering of that maiden, the rainy month of *Savan*, into the most profound depths of my soul. The sound of an insistent knocking on the door was making my half-slumbering consciousness feel transported to a vale of notes, beats and melodies. The gift of song and light rained down. Then my eyes fell upon that body carved from my dreams — that body so desired by my thirsting existence my eyes drank up the sight of it drop by drop.

She was lushly verdant — a twenty-four or twenty-five year old woman. When I saw her for the first time in a wet saffron-coloured knee-length dress I felt as though a princess from the Arabian Nights had climbed the silvery stairs of the seven heavens to alight in the vacant courtyard of my heart. The freezing blood in my veins was illuminated by the shining rays of her dazzling beauty. Her heavy-lidded eyes were filled with the magic of the *Samiri* and her vivacious body exuded the fragrance of wild flowers. When I saw her I felt as though wild poppies had bloomed in the desert of my existence.

Shonali had come to Mumbai with her crippled husband and two children to douse the fire in their bellies. She quickly became a part of the frantic life on Mira Road. Wherever she went, people could not help but stare at the curves of her sensuous body ... but she would merely ignore the hordes of admirers and gracefully go on her way. She lived in a room in Hyderi Chowk with her family. She rose at dawn and prepared the day's meals. She left for work by seven after washing up and bathing. She had carefully selected a few households to work for, among which mine was one.

She was born in Chittagong, in a remote coastal village, to a fisherman's home. Her father, Sharfuddin, was an uncommonly handsome man. His steely arms were full of might. He would unfurl his sails before dawn and go out fishing, battling the ferocious waves as he made his way into deep waters.

That day, black clouds had overshadowed the sky. It looked like a rainstorm was on its way. The god of the sea, Neptune, hissed like a python. The tempestuous waves reached to the sky. Sharfuddin's wife was soon to give birth. There was nothing in the house but a few grains of rice. Despite his fellow fishermen's entreaties, he launched his boat into the raging waves of the sea. The battle between man and sea lasted hours in that devastating storm, but Sharfuddin was victorious. The uncommon strength of his arms of steel brought him success. The valuable *shonar* fish was trapped in his net.

His fellow fishermen welcomed him with a song of man's victory over the sea. Among these was the elder, the headman of the village, who also gave him the glad tidings that with the morning's first rays, two daughters — like gold and silver — had made an auspicious visit to his home. What immense good fortune for him! The newborn babes were named Shonali and Rupali. They had come as heralds of prosperity. Their home was filled with heaps of rice. The coconut trees also stretched and grew into their prime. They felt as though fruits and flowers were raining down upon them.

Then time took another turn, and their smiling, happy life wrapped itself in a veil of sorrow. In the war of 1971, men became beasts. Massacres were commonplace. Women were robbed of their honour. People were mown down like so many carrots and radishes. The soldiers invaded the fishermen's villages. They set fire to their bamboo huts. They destroyed their coconut trees. Sharfuddin and his wife were among the dead, but it was really by a miracle of divine intervention that the newborn babies, Shonali and Rupali, were found alive in a basket, where they had been sleeping peacefully among a pile of fish.

When the flood of time was arrested, the God-fearing and compassionate people of the village managed to raise Rupali and Shonali somehow or other until they grew up. Now they went from house to house in the nearby settlements with baskets on their heads selling crabs and fish and didn't return to their cottage until late in the evening. When the sea tired and silence fell, the soft melodies of folk songs sung on the *iktara* would echo in the darkness of the huts made of coconut and banana leaves. The humming and twirling of song filled the people's hearts with spiritual vision and mirth. Nazrul's entire being was imbued with the living soil of the musical scale — he who had been so tortured by the bestial soldiers that both his legs had been rendered useless. But his soul was imbued with the heavenly melodies of the soil. His ethereal songs had won over Shonali's heart, although her innumerable admirers were prepared to sacrifice their lives for just one glance. But she preferred the lame Nazrul over everyone, and after all, he was her childhood companion. They'd studied together in the Maulvi's madrasa until class five.

Shonali loved Rupali more than life, and could not bear to be separated from her for even a moment. Even during the marriage ceremony, she kept Rupali by her side, and had her all dressed up just like herself. She had ordered a seven-yard sari of red muslin from Dhaka for Rupali and a golden satin blouse. It was hard to tell which of the two was the bride ... and on top of that, she also hung silver earrings in her ears and gave her a silver nose-ring as well, which Nazrul's family had made especially for the bride.

A river of tears flowed from Shonali's eyes at the time of the farewell. All she could do was worry about how Rupali would sleep without her.

Shonali: Faiyaz Riffat

At the end of the wedding night she didn't even pause to glance in the mirror, but tore off to her hut in the early hours of dawn, where she was deeply alarmed to see that Rupali's straw bed lay empty. She began to scream and weep. The entire village gathered when they heard her lament. People fanned out all the way to the nearby villages. They searched high and low, but Rupali was nowhere to be found. A report was filed with the police. Nazrul and Shonali even went to Kolkata. They searched in the dark and narrow lanes of the Sonagachi red light district and returned defeated.

I have given Shonali the spare key to my automatic door. She softly opens the door to the flat early in the morning and comes inside. She waters the rose bushes humming a folk song in her honeyed tones all the while. She washes the tea things. She lights the burner and warms the milk and makes the bed tea. She fills the kettle with tea and sets it on the teapoy. She rouses me with the jingling of her bangles. Despite being awake, I continue to lie still with my eyes closed. She sits at the head of the bed and places my head in her lap and massages it. I smile and stretch and sit up and place my hands on her soft thighs. She says nothing, just smiles. An intoxicating blend of bliss and pleasure spreads over me and she stands up gathering her glittering body to her.

'Sahib! Drink your tea quickly before it gets cold!' She picks up the teacup and fills it with the burgundy liquid. I sip the tea. She picks up the fresh newspaper and brings it over and places it in my lap, keeping up a constant patter of conversation.

'Why do these newspaper people print photos of half-naked women? Do these women feel no shame at all? What do they get out of showing off their bodies?' She wafts out of the bedroom like a puff of breeze. The soliloquy continues... "Oh my, there's still clothing to wash, clothing to iron, breakfast to make ... you should eat fewer eggs or you won't be able to sleep at night!'

I drink my tea, light a cigarette, then stub it out in the ashtray after a couple of puffs. Shonali expresses displeasure at my smoking. She takes the cigarettes from the packet and divides them into two sections, while confidently asserting her authority. 'You may not smoke more than half of these. I've cleaned the bathroom, it's time to get up! I have to get breakfast ready as well now.'

She lovingly makes the toast, boils the egg, and prepares lunch and dinner. Sometimes she also makes chicken along with the daal, vegetables and salad, but not more than twice a week. I bathe and emerge from the bathroom. She gets a towel and dries the droplets of water from my tousled white hair and tells me to lie down in bed. She pours some almond oil into her palm and rubs it into my hair. Then she undoes the button of my night-suit top and rubs Nivea Body Care lotion into my face, neck and chest. My body is warmed by a flame of light. But despite realising how I feel, she carries on silently with her work. As though nothing has happened at all. I am an old man of sixty-six. But she leads me about by the finger like a child. Sometimes I stretch my body and point my index finger toward my feet. Without saying a word, she sits down cross-legged near my leg. She starts off massaging my heels, then the calves, then scoots up on her knees and presses her whole weight against my thighs. When I begin to moan softly, she laughs and says, 'You're feeling pain, or does it feel good?' I stay silent, and feeling abashed, cover my face with a newspaper to hide my emotions. She rises and goes into the kitchen to cook. This is her daily routine. She carefully places the food in the fridge, and as she leaves she repeats all her advice. 'Eat on time ... and yes ... don't forget to take your blood pressure medication.' She gets to the door but then comes back. 'You're running out of spices, you need to send for mustard oil as well.' Then she opens the cupboard and takes out the money herself. 'I've taken out the money for groceries. I locked the cupboard back up and put the key under the mattress. Shall I go now, Baba?' I say all right, half-heartedly, and Shonali leaves.

I pass the time until afternoon in reading. When evening falls in the room, I go out for a jog. The whole time I think only of Shonali and feel ashamed of myself. I return home. I put on my night-suit and sprawl out on the bed. I read Marquez or Milan Kundera until I begin to doze off. As soon as my eyelids droop, a dream collage of faces soothes my existence.

A light rain began to fall. It was growing darker. My health had been poor since morning. Shonali had told the doctor of my condition and brought medicine, but I had not improved much. It was difficult to tell what time of night it was. Then I felt as though someone was placing cold compresses on my burning body. I had no idea when I fell asleep.

When my eyes opened in the morning I was astonished. Shonali was scrunched up asleep in one corner of the double bed. I had no idea what time she had come at night and finding me in a state of acute fever stayed by my side, applying cold compresses to my forehead. Suddenly she stretched and opened her eyes and sat up startled. Shrinking into her curvy body she placed her hand on my forehead. She picked up the thermometer which was in a glass, shook it, washed it, and put it in my mouth ... after waiting one minute, she looked at the temperature and said, 'Your fever has gone down, Sahib. You were delirious. Who knows what you were muttering all night. You said my name again and again and called out to me, even though I was right by your side, on this very bed. Your whole body was shaking. I held you to my chest like a baby all night long. Why don't you ask someone to come stay with you? Who will look after you when I'm gone?'

Shonali burst into tears as she said this. I also felt agitated. She wiped away her tears and began to laugh, then darted from the bedside and floated out of the room.

She returned soon, and told me, 'The doctor will come to see you. I told him how you were, and brought medicine. Take this dose now. I cooked vermicelli for you. You should take it with milk. That's all you should have for breakfast. I'll come back when I'm done at the other houses. I've told my husband.'

By evening my health had improved quite a bit. I got up and made myself some coffee and sat down with two days worth of newspapers which I hadn't had a chance to read. As I read, my eyes dropped shut and I slept for a while. At some point in the night, Shonali opened the automatic door herself and entered the bedroom. She touched my body in various places checking for fever, and feeling reassured she said, 'Eat daal soup with bread crusts. I'll make it for you. Get something in your stomach. When it's time for bed, drink some warm milk, then go to sleep. Your sickness is loneliness. I'm here today, but what of tomorrow? The police are making our lives difficult. I've searched all of Mumbai for Rupali — from Kamathipura to Peela House and Bhandup — I've looked for her in every single brothel but I haven't found her. Since the bomb explosion in the local train the police have been driving Bangladeshis away. The police have already taken my husband twice! If you hadn't paid the bribe, what would I do? Who has enough money to pay off the darned police? Okay, now, you turn over and go to sleep; close your eyes. I'll massage you with cologne; you'll relax and fall asleep.

When my eyes opened in the morning she was sleeping peacefully with me in her arms, a light smile on her lips.

Then I fell into a storm of doldrums as I wondered if this tulip of the desert would ever have the chance to find what she was looking for.

—*Translated by Daisy Rockwell*

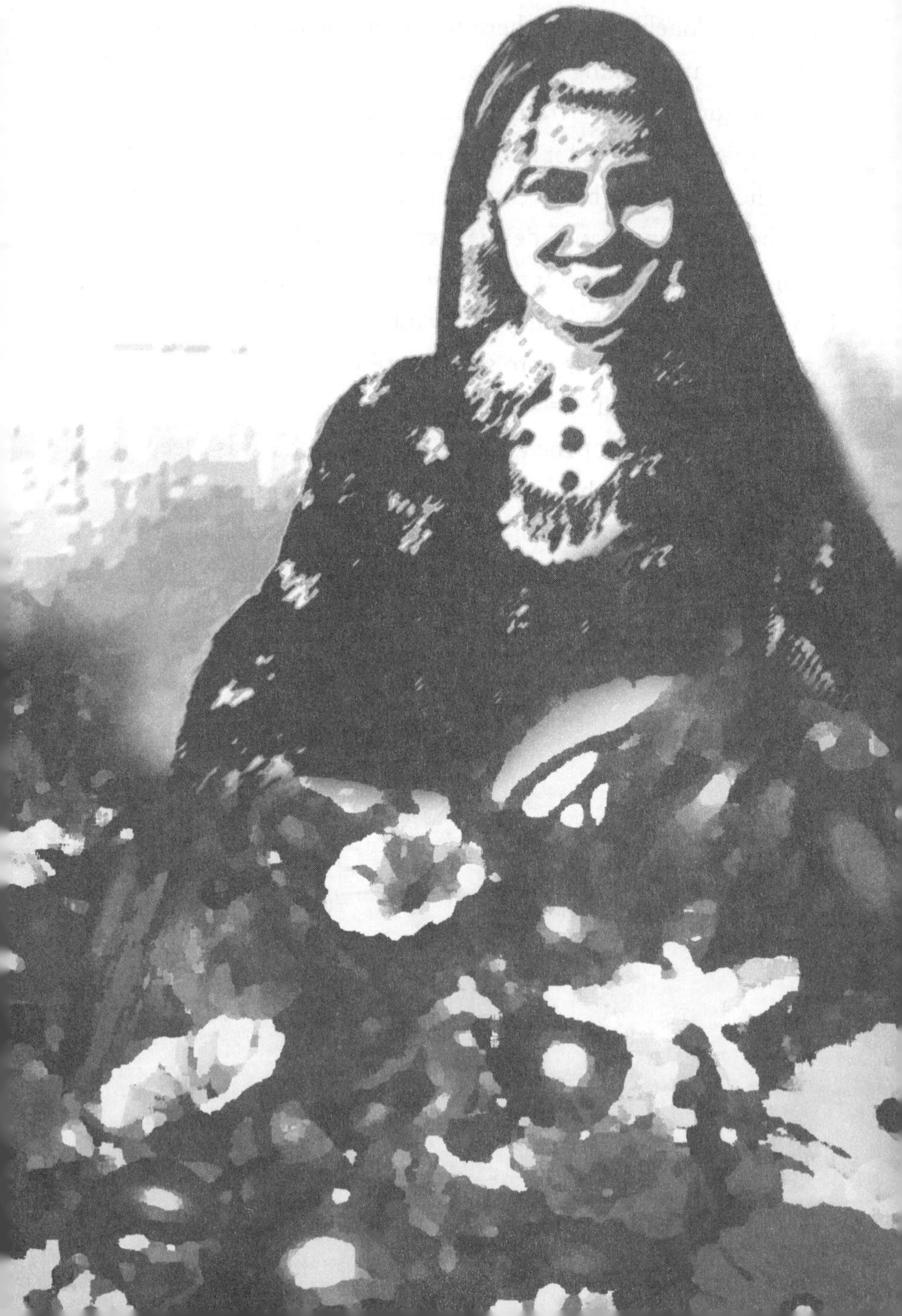

Wedding Night

Ratan Singh

The girl who tended the gardens went to pluck some flowers for her wedding night. The garden seemed delighted to behold her great beauty! The branches of flower-bearing trees seemed to reach out to her grasp. The buds seemed to giggle with joy and the flowers seemed to become even more fragrant with happiness.

First, there was the fragrance of the flowers and then there was the fragrance from her body! The air was heady with the mingled perfume of both and in the words of Waris Shah, 'the news of the gardener's daughter's impending nuptials and the flowers that needed to be plucked, spread in the world.' Rose, magnolia, jasmine, narcissus, 'queen of the night'...you could name any flowering bush and they would all be swaying in unison, with pleasure. They seemed to move their branches towards her, as if to embrace her.

If she moved towards the roses, the chrysanthemums would lean forwards and clamour for her attention.

Nubile buds nestled together and giggled shyly, vying with one another to place themselves in the girl's basket.

The bees were perplexed. 'Where should they go!' The fragrant floral display or the enticing beauty of the girl whose garden it was. The velvety softness of the flower beds or the girl's sweet breath?

As she continued to pick the flowers, she laughed and the flowers were mesmerised by her and her body, in turn, became radiant amidst these flowers. The individual scents from the flowers mingled with her body to create a special musk.

That very musk, which when it awakens in a doe's being, makes it lovelorn and mad with desire. It tries to find the source of that fragrance, without avail and darts about aimlessly in its pursuit, only to fall in the clutches of a male deer.

A magical spell and a lustful web.

A spell that entranced her.

A sharp dagger.

A dagger that slices a body apart.

And digs itself deeper and deeper in the body.

Something similar happened with this girl. As the fragrance of musk formed in her body, a fire lit within her, whose radiance reached the Sun-God. She felt her body being engulfed in these flames of passion. The Sun-God leapt to reach the girl and his eyes widened in disbelief.

She was even more beautiful than the wife of Sage Gautam, who had enticed God Indra. The Sun-God contemplated her great beauty and approached her.

He said, 'O, garden girl, your beauty, your allure, it's all so irresistible. Give me the flowers you carry in your basket.'

The girl quickly covered her face with her veil and replied, 'O mighty Sun, my beauty, my allure, it's all for my lover who waits for me in anticipation of our wedding night. And so I cannot give you my flowers.'

But the Sun-God was enamoured by her beauty. And within him, crackled the flames of lust. He was crazed with desire. And

Wedding Night: Ratan Singh

so did not hear the woman's refusal. Or if he heard it, he paid no heed. A man's wishes are paramount and even the Sage's wife, Ahilya, had not been spared, so what of this poor girl who tends the garden? The lust of the body overtook the mind and led the Sun-God down the path of wrongdoing.

To further his wishes, he played a cruel trick. He assumed the appearance of her fiancé, the gardener, and appeared before her. The girl was taken aback. She gazed at him shyly and then spread her arms to embrace him warmly. She showered him with love and affection and was deliriously happy.

She whispered, 'You have no patience. You did not wait for me!'

Saying that, she continued to shower the Sun-God with her pure love and, unwittingly, satiated his lust. She gave him her precious basket of flowers and asked him to go home. She planned to bathe in the lake and follow him later.

As she quickly made her way home after her bath, she saw her fiancé, the gardener. Seeing her empty basket of flowers, his heart sank as he saw the prospect of his wedding night slip away.

He asked, 'Why is your basket empty? Did you misplace your flowers?'

The girl stayed quiet.

What could she say? How could she reveal what had befallen her?

Once the truth was apparent to both, he said, 'O keeper of my gardens, Ahilya has been duped again. You have been tricked, dearest, you have been tricked.'

Saying this, he fell quiet and went into deep thought. He began to murmur, 'Ahilya's husband was a great sage and she willingly gave herself to God Indra. And I ... I ... I am just an ordinary gardener. I cannot take him to task.' He was lost in thought and kept saying meaningless things. As he continued with his ruminations, a strange venom seeped into the girl's body and, like Ahilya, she began to turn into a statue made of stone.

As the gardener saw his beloved turn to stone, he quickly shook her and exclaimed, 'No, dearest, no. Don't turn to stone. Ram had to come to bring Ahilya back to life. Who will come to bring you back? No, No, I will not give up. We will not be defeated. We will celebrate our wedding night. This time you stay at home. I will go and pluck the flowers from the garden.'

As he reached the edge of the garden, the flowering branches looked upon him with the same ecstasy and eagerness. Today his labours would be rewarded. Today the creator of this garden has come to collect his rewards. The flowers were ready to grant him his wish. Soon his basket was full to the brim. As soon as the basket was full of flowers, the gardener's body imbibed their fragrance and a nymph, Menaka, happened to be passing by. Her heart fluttered. She called out, 'I am a fairy from the heavens. My beauty is all-encompassing. The intoxication of your love fills me with a glow. You are mine. O, give me the fragrance of your flowers.'

Menaka smiled and came towards the gardener, 'My heart is filled with desire. O gardener, put all the flowers of your love in my basket.'

As she advanced towards him, the gardener stepped back, shaking his head, in refusal. 'My wife-to-be is the queen of my heart. These flowers symbolise her love for me. Tonight is a special night, we will celebrate together. You are a mad woman. I will not give you my precious flowers.'

Wedding Night: Ratan Singh

Menaka was heartbroken and his words enraged her. She cried out, 'My allure is legendary. Even sages have not been able to resist me. You are a mere gardener!'

As she contemplated what to do, she waved her sparkling scarf in the air and turned herself into the gardener's beloved and appeared before him.

Then she proceeded to take aim and directed the arrow of lust from her bow.

When the gardener saw his beloved, he ran towards her.

'Why such impatience? My dearest, could you not wait?'

Menaka smiled inwardly and went to embrace him.

What does the gardener know?

He has been duped.

When the gardener's lover saw him return without any flowers, she was crestfallen. Her dreams of the wedding night were flowing away like water.

On the face of it, this story is about the gardener and his betrothed.

But it is a universal story from the days of yore, one that is familiar to all.

The gardener and his beloved even today dream of the joys of their wedding night in their lifetime. They grow flowers. They carefully pick flowers. But the wedding night eludes them.

The dawn of happiness has not yet happened.

—Translated by Tabinda J. Burney

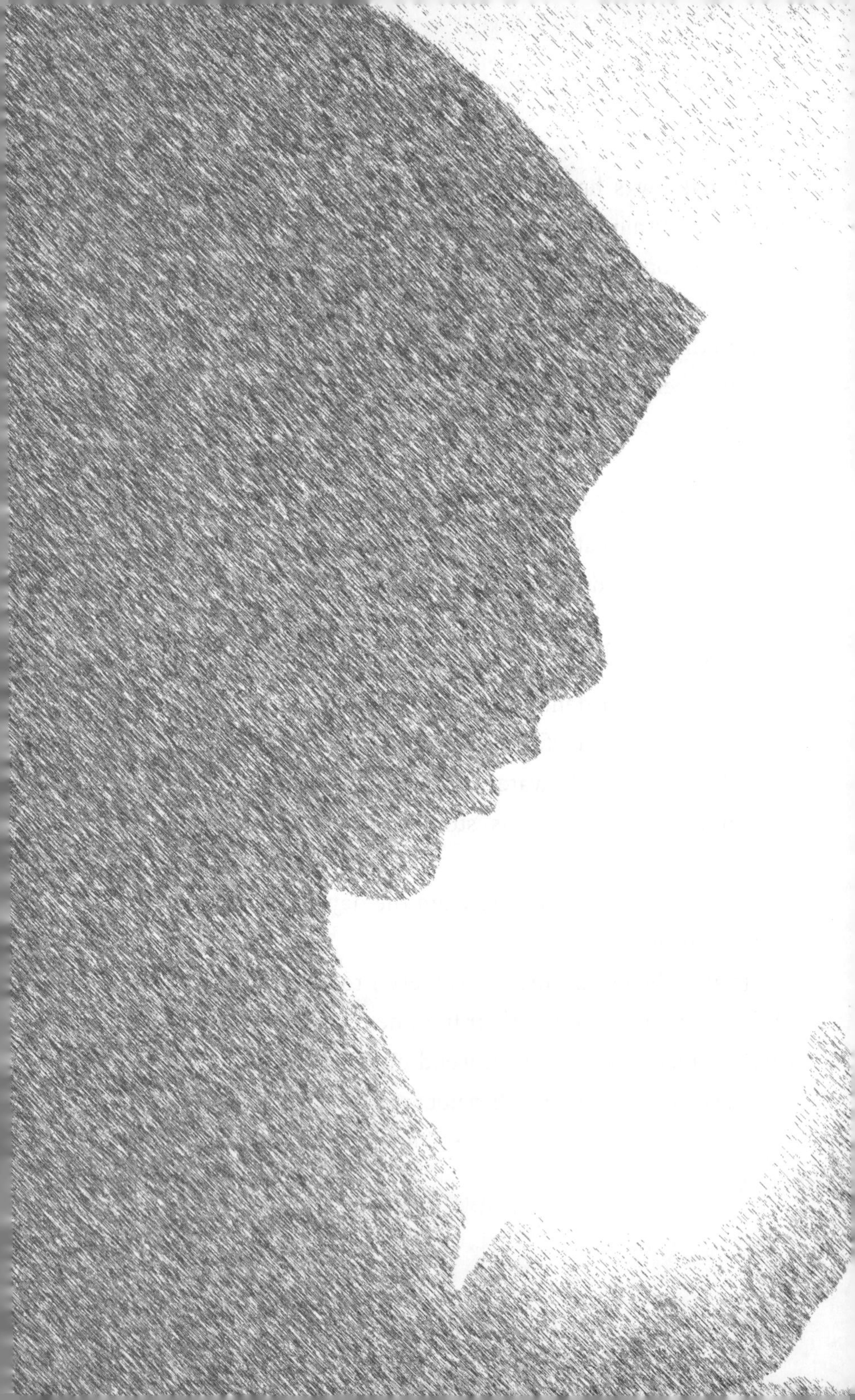

The Heavy Stone

Baig Ehsas

The bottle of nail polish kept on the dressing table startled her. She glanced towards the calendar; the month was drawing to a close and she had not painted her nails yet.

So what?

'You can't do your *wuzoo* if you have put on nail polish.' Her grandmother had told her and had immediately removed it from her nails. Particular about *namaz* herself, her grandmother wouldn't let her miss any either. Still, she found find an opportunity to put it at night and, just before the pre-dawn *fajr* prayer, she would clean her nails before she went for the ritual ablutions. She knew she could ruin her nails in this fashion but such was her fascination with nail colours that she could not help herself. One day when she suddenly started bleeding, shaking with fear, she crawled into her grandmother's lap for shelter who explained the phenomena to her. Having eased her qualms, she told her granddaughter to forego *namaz* during her menstrual cycle. She painted her nails while her grandmother sat smiling.

On the one hand, she was elated to be painting her nails and on the other, she was faced with the fair share of problems that came with it. Not saying her prayers made her feel as if she was missing out on something. The sound of every *azaan* would make her jump out of her skin but the sight of her nails would make her smile. On those days, she felt reluctant to step out of the house. Those days were strange and foul smelling, leaving her feeling rather sluggish with a severe pain in her limbs. She spent the entire day crawled up in her grandmother's lap. Not only did this bring a halt to all parties and visits to her girlfriends but it also resulted in skipping school, sometimes. She stared at her painted nails all day long; they were indeed quite beautiful.

So soon, so much had changed. Jumping and skipping beauty queens on television would shamelessly reveal covert secrets which nobody seemed to mind. Children as well as adults would remain unfazed.

With the passing away of her grandmother, her fear of such days also seemed to fade away. Yet, she continued to paint her nails. Her painted nails served as a reminder of her day-off from *namaz*.

So what?

A wave of happiness washed over her. If this is so, then what an unusual coincidence. Since their marriage, they had only met for one night and this was a memento of her marital status. If the baby were to be born, she would celebrate its birthday along with her wedding anniversary. She could do so since she knew exactly when her baby was actually conceived. How many women get such an opportunity? Such a clue is never really unearthed. No one truly ever knows which child is the outcome of which time period; only she could tell. She smiled and gently stroked her abdomen. Strangely, she could almost feel a little bump forming.

'All ready?' She giggled. As her fingers reached her navel, she felt something move inside her. A faint noise called out to her:

The Heavy Stone: Baig Ehsas

'Mummy!' She was startled. Yes, this voice was emanating from her navel. She wanted to rest her ear on her navel in order to listen closely. How would this be possible? You needed another person to listen in such a way. She would make him listen to this voice when she met him in the evening.

As she left the house, she took every step with great caution. It became difficult to concentrate on her work and all day long she avoided those around her. Several times in the course of the day, she heard that delicate noise calling out to her: 'Mummy, Mummy!'

Lovingly she scolded it, 'Hush ... be quiet.' Afraid that her colleagues might also hear the sound, she missed lunch as she wanted him to be the first person to hear it.

He came right on time to meet her. It was always the same routine ... from office to the park, to sit in the park till dusk, to roam on the streets... to eat in restaurants ... to watch any movie in the theatres ... absolutely any movie — be it in English, Hindi, Telugu — the sole purpose being to spend time together. They had both grown tired of this situation. Despite being a married couple, they had to sneak around like lovers ... to be the victim of several suspicious looks ... it had all become so hurtful ... although they had got married they did not have a home of their own to go to and he used to drop her back at her house each night. How she wished for a home of their own that he could take her to! They would have gone home and she would have undraped her sari and asked him to put his ear to her navel to listen to that delicate voice.... 'Mummy!'

She sat cautiously on the seat of the scooter and wondered why she felt as if he were driving rashly, today of all days. She

69

found the streets to be unusually uneven. Though he did not ever drive impulsively, he reduced his speed even more today.

As they reached their special spot in the park, the sun was setting behind the branches of a tree. The last of the sunlight filtered through the leaves in slanting stripes. A heap of dry leaves were being burnt nearby. Smoke was rising and a peculiar smell filled the air. A kite had perched herself on a dry branch of a high tree and was constantly keening. Her male counterpart was circling overhead like an aeroplane waiting for a landing signal.

At that moment, he put his hand on her waist. She knew that slowly his fingers would stop at her navel and he would feel her little bump just around her midriff — and that is just what he did. He felt as if his child would suffocate, so he removed his hand.

'Why?' he asked astonished.

'Place your ear here.' He did so.

'Can you hear anything?'

'What do you mean?' As if he understood everything, she blushed and waited for him to kiss her. But he was serious. All of a sudden, the sun dipped even lower. A ray touched her cheek, a flame sparked.

'Aren't you happy?'

'No, it is not that ... but given our condition, you know....'

'If I tell you something, you will jump with joy.'

'Tell me.'

'This is a memento of our *suhaag raat*, such a gift is so rare, isn't it?' she said it an impassioned tone but he did not stir.

'I will carry it,' she said it with conviction...

'But how will we manage? We do not have a house. Apart from a few friends, no one knows of our marriage. We are not even financially strong to arrange things immediately. Your medical bills ... your job ... plus your mother will throw you out of the house.... how will we manage?' He was worried.

'I will take care of everything.'

'Be practical, my love ... I am not able to think straight ... what is the hurry? We have not even straightened ourselves out yet....' he tried to explain.

'We will not be able to straighten ourselves out all our lives,' she retorted, tears welling up in her eyes. She was not expecting such a reaction. In a sudden gust, the flames sparked in the heap of half-burnt leaves.

'Please, try and understand what I am saying....' He cupped her face in his hands but she jerked his hands away.

The sun was setting. The sky was a burning red coal. In its redness, branches and tree trunks seemed almost blackish, as if they were shadows.

'Listen to me, the world has changed so much. The circle is now complete. Before civilisation, men lived like animals. There was no concept of personal property. Then came the dawn of personal property. Families were formed, clans were formed, and so were relationships.... Man was now happy with his family. Then this family became a burden. A new concept of nuclear family sprung up. He could not even tolerate that and embarked on contract marriages.... Now he simply could not make do with the concept of marriage even and with that men and women indulged in physical relations at their whim....'

'Despite this children are born and no means of precaution is fully effective, these children take birth too.' She pointed out with bitterness.

'Yes, but they have found a solution to this. There are places called "Child Farms" and children are left at such places.'

'Just like poultry farms — so the child does not know who its parents are! I did not know you were one of those people who refuse to differentiate between the offspring of a hen and a human,' she spoke angrily.

'That was not my intention, my love; I too want a child but this is not the time. What sort of a life can we offer it? Just wait for some time.'

'If you insist on an abortion I will get a hysterectomy to go with it.'

'What do you mean?'

'You can go ahead and mate with whoever you want and leave your child at a Child Farm!'

'Listen!'

'Shut up!' she retorted and stood up. Swiftly, both walked out of the park. As she sat on the scooter, she neither touched his thigh nor leaned on him. Usually, she would sit so close to him that passersby would turn around to look at them. By now he was used to feeling the warmth of her body on his back; but whenever she was annoyed with him she would maintain a distance. He knew it was symbolic of her annoyance. They did not talk to each other the entire way. She marched off to her house as soon as she got off the scooter. She did not even ask him when he would be coming tomorrow. Disappointed, he waited for a while and then left.

As soon as she reached her room, she collapsed on the bed without changing her clothes. He seemed an entirely different person today. He gave no importance to the talk about the child

The Heavy Stone: Baig Ehsas

being a memento of their *suhaag raat*. We will bear a child later. Child Farm! How easy is it to philosophise. Almost as if we are a part of the western world. Here, in India, even the next generation will not bear witness to any Child Farm. God forbid, no such thing will take place here. Our maternal and paternal grandmothers are still alive, relationships are still of great significance to us.

Gradually, she cooled down. A pile of utensils and clothes were kept in one corner. A mother's attitude! What sort of a mother was she? She has been turned into a maid. She works all day and completes the daily chores too. When will she gain freedom from this hell? They have been trying for three years before they got married but have been unsuccessful in securing a house for themselves. They are married now — but a house? Maybe he is right. How would she manage to raise a child in such an environment. Mother would throw her out of the house ... where would she go then? Where would they find a house? Who will take care of her? How will everything work out?

She picked up a *chaadar* and draped it over her head and went straight to the lady doctor.

'Is this your first baby?'

'Yes.'

'Why don't you want to keep it?'

'I want a gap.'

'Let the first baby come and then think of the gap,' the lady doctor said.

'No, ...'

The doctor prescribed some medicines which she brought.

As she picked up a glass to drink water along with the medicines, the same delicate voice called out, 'Mummy!' Her eyes welled up. She put the glass down. How he used to say that a *nishaani*, a sign was so important. His features, her colour. His voice, her accent. His mischievousness, her seriousness. His intelligence, her knowledge! Then what happened? No, he still wants it but under better conditions ... Circumstances! Circumstances! Why was the *nikaah* imperative in such circumstances? Was the *suhaag raat* also imperative? Then how did 'circumstances' come into the picture now? She writhed in anger. Just as everything has played out, this will too. But how will she be able to hide the indications of her pregnancy? Maybe that is why he refused. She swallowed the medicine. Now, that delicate voice will stop. Her heart was heavy. What an unfortunate woman she is! She will paint her nails in the morning.

But she went to the office without painting her nails. She could not concentrate on her work. He came to pick her up in the evening and wordlessly she climbed onto the back seat just like yesterday, maintaining a distance between them. They approached the park.

Sunlight still shone on the bridge. They reached the tree which had long pods hanging from its branches. When the pods burst, their red seeds would scatter all over the green lawns and look like tiny ladybirds. They had discovered this tree with great difficulty. There was only one tree of its kind in the entire park. She started gathering the red seeds. He too started collecting seeds although there were only a few seeds today. By now, they had reached the bridge.

'Are you angry with me?' he asked.

'Why would you think so?'

'You probably did not like my attitude yesterday.'

'Let's not talk about it. We will do as you wish. We will have no baby.'

'When did I say that?'

'But I have decided that I will get a hysterectomy done along with the abortion.'

'You will do no such thing!'

'I will do as I wish!'

'Why are you being so stubborn?' he asked, sounding irritated. 'All right then, don't do anything, just carry it.'

'For your information, I have already met with a lady doctor and taken the pills she had prescribed.'

'Oh!' with that he fell silent.

There was a long silence after that. In order to break the tension in the air, he brought up the topic of a TV serial. With that they started talking about movies and their jobs. Yet, it was all so artificial and shallow. The prescription pills were now over; she waited for as many days as the doctor had asked to but the voice calling out 'Mummy, Mummy' continued to ring in her ears. She met with the lady doctor again.

'Keep it; it seems stubborn,' said the lady doctor.

'No,' she said firmly.

She was injected this time. She could feel the injection sting all over her body. Her child would now die. She was restless all night. Like every day, they reached the park in the evening. This time she did not share her feelings or her thoughts.

There was smoke on the bridge. They sat on the bench by the artificial lake. This lake was made for boating. It was flanked by coconut trees on both the sides. The water in the lake was muddy. Dirt had accumulated on one side. Frogs were swimming on the surface of the water. As they slapped their webbed feet on the water, circles would form and scatter one by one. Whenever a boat passed by, its waves crushed all the circles. Soon, the energetic frogs would engage themselves in making circles once again.

He held her hand quietly. He noticed her nails; they were not painted. She leaned on his shoulder. What sort of a tension is this! Had circumstances been slightly better then maybe this tension would not have existed. They would have welcomed their first child with joy. She was right: it is rather unusual to know just when a baby is conceived.

'Are you tense?' he asked lovingly.

She looked at him softly but did not say anything.

'No, you carry it.' he said. Yet she remained silent.

This time when she sat on the back seat of his scooter, she wrapped herself around him. Neither spoke a word throughout the way.

Upon reaching her house, she lay down quietly.

'Mummy!' a delicate voice called out.

She was startled. Had the injection not worked?

She ran to the lady doctor. 'Wait for two or three days or else we will do an MTP! There is no other way.'

Three days passed, the voice continued. Nothing happened. The two did not speak on this topic either. She suffered through the pain alone. The lady doctor had given an appointment for tomorrow. She tossed and turned all night. Who knows what will happen?

'Mummy, mummy!'

Her heart sank. *Beta*, our world is not such where you can be born. Look, we do not have a house of our own. Who will look after you and me? Who will look after you when I go to work?'

'Mummy, mummy!' a voice persisted.

She was awake the whole night. She applied for a leave of absence in the morning, put some money into her purse and came to the hospital. She was frightened.

'Are you alone?'

'Yes.'

'No mother or husband?'

'It does not matter.' Her tone shocked the lady doctor.

'You did the right thing by coming early in the morning,' the doctor said almost as if trying to soothe her pain.

She was taken into the operation theatre.

'Please leave your *chappals* outside,' said the nurse. She took off her *chappals*. It was a strange feeling. Almost as if she were stepping into a butcher house. She was made to lie down. The nurse washed her legs with antiseptic and asked her to take off her clothes and change into a hospital gown. She tied her hair and covered it with a scarf. Although the room was air-conditioned, she was dripping with sweat.

'What is the matter?'

'Nothing.'

'Why are you sweating so much?' The lady doctor touched a bead of sweat from the cavity between her breasts and said, 'Think about it.'

'I have thought very deeply about it,' she spoke, her voice firm with conviction.

A nurse began searching for a vein to start a drip line. She found a vein with great difficulty. A bottle was kept beside the operating table. The doctor administered a sedative. The bottle soon seemed hazy. 'Slide down slightly,' said the doctor. Her mind was drowning. She was so lonely. There was nobody she could cry out for help.

Even after the injection was administered, she could still hear that voice.

'Mummy, mummy!'

'Mummy, mummy!'

The voice began to fade slowly. The last time she heard the voice, it was almost as if it was coming from a deep well. Soon, she was unconscious. As she regained consciousness, she realised she was alone in the room. There was a pin-drop silence in the room. Then somebody entered the room. It was the doctor. 'Rest for an hour. Once you have regained some strength, you may go home.' The doctor's voice echoed. A part of her identity was now lost. She was incomplete. Somewhere, something, was missing. She cried her heart out once the doctor left. Hours passed. When the doctor told her she was allowed to leave, she stumbled away. Once home, she went straight to lie down in her room. The bottle of nail polish was kept on the dressing table. She picked it up to paint her nails and the sticky liquid flowed down as she unscrewed the cap. The brush on her nail felt like fresh blood. Blood.... She started sobbing. She felt as though her child had been pushed into a deep well.

The Heavy Stone: Baig Ehsas

Maybe he is safe now. A caravan passing by will help pull him out of the well.... Then he will run through seven locked doors which unlock on their own. But he will stop at the prison door. He will step out of the prison, and he will be aged. By then, she would have turned blind. Her son will lead her out of the darkness[1].

—*Translated by Aaliya Waziri with Mehjabeen Jalil*

---

1   The reference here seems to be to Yusuf (the Biblical Joseph), son of Yaqub (Jacob) who is not only extremely good looking but also has the gift of interpreting dreams. His envious brothers throw him in a well from where he is rescued by a passing caravan, sold to an Egyptian and eventually, after facing many hardships, rises to a position of eminence in the pharaoh's court. The story of Yusuf is narrated in the 12th chapter, the Surah Yusuf, in the Quran and holds great emotional appeal for Muslims for it tells of an exceedingly beautiful and gifted child who, after many travails, brings succour and relief to his parents in their old age through his steadfast belief in God.—Editor

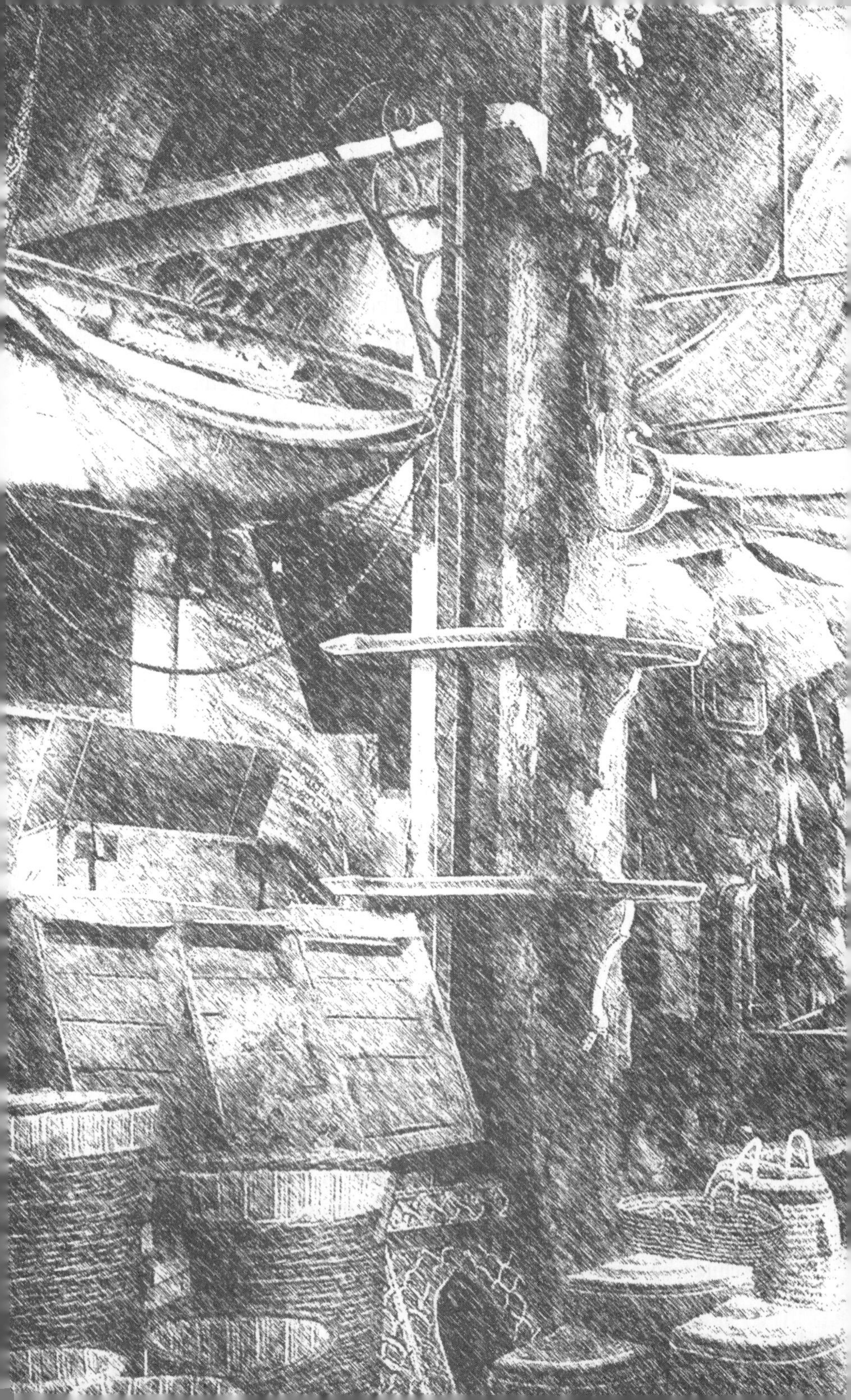

Awaiting the Zephyr

Syed Muhammad Ashraf

As the doctor entered the settlement, he noticed a series of wide front stoops along both sides of the street all leading towards a building made of thin, old-fashioned white-washed bricks. These tall stoops were piled high with all manner of goods such that the observer might guess their price without even asking. The hale and hearty merchants seated alert before their shops selling the goods represented a variety of hues and ethnicities. This sequence of shops did not end when it reached the white brick building, but rather continued for some distance in a different direction, with similar stoops arranged with a variety of wares. Sturdily built men wandered about along the roadside rattling the metal bowls clutched in their hands as they sprinkled the ground with water from the leather satchels slung across their shoulders. Shoppers, attired in clothing of all different colours, tribes and groups, walked about from shop to shop. The street was filled with the sounds of all sorts of voices — sweet, soft, harsh, sputtering, gloomy, joyful.

The walls of the white brick building were not of unscaleable height. Doors were cut into the walls here and there, and windows and latticed ventilation grates, through which the ceaselessly echoing tumult coming from the bazaar could easily be heard. Standing below and listening to those voices it seemed as though they had bodies, and as though those bodies were adorned with long, silky-white beards and flowing tresses that fell in waves till below the ears. On hearing those voices, one felt the same sort of peace one might on discovering a cool jug of fragrant water from which to drink to one's fill after undertaking a journey on foot for miles in a scorching summer breeze. This serene building with low walls was surrounded on all sides by pillars, turrets, minarets and gates that gave one the impression of a palace. But try as one might, it would really be quite difficult to ascertain if the bazaar surrounded this white building or if the bazaar was an exterior portion of the white building or if the two were undivided portions of the same becolumned and minarated edifice. All three of these were connected and continuous, like the original tracings on an old map. Occasionally sharp voices from within the palace-like building would pour out for a short while, and even drown out the sounds emanating from the white building and the chattering tumult of the bazaar. Sometimes this would occur for protracted interludes. Then suddenly it would also happen that the voices in the bazaar would rise to the level of loud whispers, then many voices would join together and reverberate, and the white building's ethereal intonations would mingle with the cries from the bazaar and drown out all the voices in the palace.

 The doctor adjusted his sacred thread, felt for the stethoscope around his neck and tightly clutching his bag, entered a rectangular room that was situated right in the middle of the settlement. He hesitated for a moment, then slowly acclimatised to the silent, mournful atmosphere in the room. Perhaps he was also a bit frightened on observing the immense beauty of his surroundings. In the middle of the room lay a large, lovely round-legged bed, with a black headboard worked in intricate designs. The bed was laid with rich and splendid linens and quilts, and upon these linens lay a woman. She was tall and extremely beautiful. Her hair was golden as that of women of the Turkish race, and gave no hint as to her age. Her brow was clear and her nose delicate and regal. Her eyes were half-opened and kohl-lined. Her cheeks were pink, despite her illness. Her rosy lips too were half-parted, revealing pearl-white teeth that glittered like stars with the rise and fall of her breathing. Her smooth neck was traced with fine blue veins, and the feminine attributes below her neck were high and conical. Her fair wrists rested beside full hips. The doctor stared hard at her hands and feet and had a strange sensation that their fullness betrayed a habituation to labour. But care had also been taken to keep them clean and soft. The invalid's breathing was irregular; for several moments her body would appear still, and then suddenly, with a jerk, the uneven breathing would begin again.

A tall man, whose head and hair were covered with a pointed cap, stood by the side of the bed. A magnificent but uneven beard adorned his elderly pink and white complexion, and dignity and elegance shone from his eyes. By his demeanour and attire he seemed by turns an emperor or a dervish. The doctor stood on the other side of the bed, his head lowered before the man with respect.

The doctor continued to gaze at the invalid for some time. The man stared fixedly at her with worried eyes. All of a sudden, the doctor felt as though this large room was surrounded by many other curtained off rooms, and that from behind these curtains the jangling of bangles, mournful whispers and suppressed sighs could be discerned. From some rooms, new-born babies kicked up a fuss with their cries. Whenever the sound of these voices grew louder, lines of displeasure formed on the brow of the tall man. The doctor felt that the audible whispers from behind the curtains were nearly comprehensible, though not connected to any one language.

After a brief pause the doctor felt he needed to know about the relationship between the gentleman and the lady in order to understand more about her.

'How is she ... related to you?'

'She is much beloved by me.'

'Pardon me?'

'By beloved, I mean I have the greatest respect and love for her.'

'But what is her connection to you?'

'I am indeed her Earthly Lord.'

The doctor stared at him with wide-open eyes. A speaker of standard Hindi, he was unable to understand the man's ornate Urdu. Then he cleared his throat and said, 'As a doctor, I should know what illness the patient suffers from. In order to know about the illness it is also necessary to ask your relation to her as well. The connection you are telling me I am unable to understand.'

The tall man smiled with pain. 'Please enquire and I will enlighten you with all it is I know to the best of my capabilities.'

From the doctor's facial expression one had the impression that despite his imperfect understanding of the flowery phrasing, he realised that this gentleman knew quite a bit, or perhaps everything, about the patient.

'How long has she been in this condition?'

'It has been many moons.'

There was a long silence, which was exaggerated by the whispers in that same understandable but unfamiliar tongue from the next rooms.

The tall man read on the doctor's face discomfort, and this time he began to share a few details.

'Belovèd — I mean the patient — has not touched victuals to her mouth in quite some time. Household remedies have been brought to her lips, but have not reached her stomach. The invalid never speaks of her ailment. Sometimes her skin turns red with fever. If you lay your hands upon her, in just a short while her body grows damp and cold as ice and feels as though all traces of life are coming to an end. The anomalism of her respiration is our greatest cause for concern.'

'The what of her respiration?' asked the doctor.

'The anomalism, that is to say, the irregularity, of her respiration, her breathing.'

The doctor took a deep breath and asked hesitantly, 'May I place my stethoscope on the patient and check?'

'Certainly. The patient has never observed purdah.'

The patient's breathing was relatively normal at that time. The doctor pulled her ornate dupatta to one side and placing his stethoscope on her chest, listened attentively. His eyes opened wide with astonishment. He quickly removed the device and tried to listen to the faint voices bubbling up from every corner of the room. Yet there was no other sound in the room but her breathing. He reapplied the device. He again evinced surprise. For a long time he listened, stethoscope to her chest, eyes closed. As long as the instrument remained in place, the invalid's face was wreathed in contentment. The doctor again removed the stethoscope and spoke in an agitated tone.

'The patient's heart is in very good condition. There's no sign of any kind of illness.'

The tall man's face betrayed no sign of surprise.

'Are you not surprised?'

'No.' The reply was succinct. The doctor had not expected this answer but he controlled himself, and emphasising each and every word, he explained, 'What I am going to tell you will astonish you very much when you hear it. There are waves of music coming from the patient's heart; I have heard them several times.'

The tall man smiled with faint dignity and softly nodded in agreement.

The doctor was stunned at the tall man's composure, but he continued with his train of thought.

'The tune that springs from her heart — it contains the burbling of a brook. And the mellifluous rustling of the breeze, and the chirping of birds.'

The tall man raised a hand to stop him. The doctor felt as though he had become lost in nostalgic thoughts. Then he spoke:

'No doubt you detected in the tune the vibration of the first blow to the war drum in the field of battle. And when two bodies in love first meet and experience one another through the lips — that soft sound of delight must also have been present. You must have heard the echo of the ecstatic cry of the Sufi clad in sandal-hued robes as well. And the growl of the emperor in his court, when he has handed down his judgment in a case of blood money. The calls of songbirds heralding the arrival of spring in the desert — that too — and the sound of the first droplets of the monsoon as they fall upon barren lands. And the harp, the sitar, and the tabla.' He fell silent.

'Yes. Those sorts of sounds — but it's hard to put into words,' said the doctor.

Suddenly a young boy popped in from a room next door, and asked in casual Hindi, 'They're asking inside about what sickness the doctor says for the lady.'

As soon as she heard this voice, the patient's colouring changed and her breathing became irregular all at once. A haze of loathing pervaded the countenance of the tall man.

'Go inside. Go inside. Watch it! Don't you set foot in here without permission!'

The young boy looked at him with surprise and went back inside.

The doctor ran his fingers through the patient's golden hair to the roots in a combing motion, and rested his palm on her cranium.

'Her fever is increasing,' he muttered. His hand was damp from the perspiration on her forehead as he reached toward her eyes. He pushed up one eyelid slowly with his thumb. The white of her eye sparkled. He felt the heat from her cheek with the back of his hand, and mumbled softly, 'Now her body is cooling down.'

The tall man's eyes flickered with anxiety; then he said in a low voice, 'The source of the disease is respiration.'

The doctor looked at him and thought a bit, then focused on the rise and fall of the patient's bosom and began to test her uneven breathing. Next he stood up straight and said with great confidence, 'The patient's entire body is full of life. The only problem is her breathing, but that problem is very grave. There's no cure for weak lungs.'

'Have you incontrovertible evidence that both lungs are ultimately inefficacious?'

When the doctor looked at him in confusion, he rephrased the question in simple language.

The doctor put on his stethoscope and examined the lungs for the first time. He listened for a long time. Then he remarked, 'It's very odd. The lungs are completely fine but she's not breathing all the way in.'

'What is the correlation between consistent respiration and the vigour of the various other parts of the body?' the tall man asked.

'There's a strong correlation. When fresh air combines with the blood via the lungs then life is created. That life mingles with the blood and gives strength to every part of the body. If we don't get enough air, then blood ... red blood very soon turns blue and illness spreads to every part of the body.'

'If you hypothesise that the lungs are functioning properly then why is there a paucity of fresh air in the body?'

'The reason why there's not enough air going into the body is that there's no fresh air in this room,' the doctor replied confidently.

'All the rest of the doors are open in the rooms that open into this room, and there are numerous windows to the outside in those rooms,' the tall man elaborated.

'But it seems to me that no fresh air is coming in through any window.'

Suddenly one of the doors to an adjacent room opened and a little girl wearing a frock entered.

'Mama is asking did the lady's fever go down or not?'

The patient's body shuddered for a moment and then her breathing became laboured again.

'Get out of here! I don't want to see your face!' exclaimed the tall man, gnashing his teeth. 'Scoundrel!' he hissed in an enraged whisper.

'Why are you angry? Mama sent me inside to find out what was happening. What did I do wrong?' the girl protested, wrinkling her nose.

The words, accent and voice of this girl seemed to render the tall man mad with rage. The doctor managed to calm him down with much difficulty. He motioned to the girl to leave the room.

Then the doctor explained, 'I have only one medicine with me. Every doctor has only one type of medicine for this type of patient. That medicine can expand the finer veins in weak lungs so that they fill with fresh air, but ...'

'But what?' the tall man asked impatiently.

'But this medicine only works when the patient has proper access to fresh air. Only then can air make its way into the expanded veins of the lungs. If there isn't any fresh air, there's no way to expand the veins.'

'Then?' the tall man asked worriedly.

'Then there's no remedy.' The doctor's tone was disconsolate. After a short silence, he asked, 'Can the patient's room not be changed?'

'No, this is Belovèd's special room. She's spent her whole life here. Many buildings and many rooms have sprung up all around over the years, but this room is for no one but Belovèd.'

'But can't you give the patient some other room besides this one? And how did she stay alive for so long without fresh air?'

'The problem of lack of fresh air is relatively recent. On all four sides of the invalid's room are rooms occupied by family members. They all have windows, ventilation slats, and doors, but the people living there don't open them.'

'Do those people have no need of leaving their rooms to visit other people?'

'No. Instead, they have forged paths inside the walls for their own ease and comfort.'

'Well, then I can't imagine how the patient has survived until now. It's quite difficult to stay alive shut up in stale air day and night.'

'Well, actually, there is one room in this house with a door that opens to the outdoors when evening falls, and a puff of air enters at that time. Perhaps this is how she sustains her existence. And then of course, Belovèd is made of very stern stuff.' The tall, handsome man looked lovingly at the woman lying on the bed as he spoke.

The doctor thought a while, then spoke:

'This is the first time I've seen a patient of this type. Can you tell me if she has any other relatives? Sometimes we inherit an illness from our forebears.'

'Belovèd has several sisters. One sister is quite elderly. She resides outside this country. She is as hearty as a young man, and is regarded with deference and veneration even outside her own country.'

'And?'

'There's one sister who's a bit older than she; she also lives outside this country, and she's very cheerful and contented in her own country. All pleasures and comforts have been written in her fate. And there's one sister in this country as well. She is quite comfortable too. That sister's in-laws wished for Belovèd to follow in her footsteps, but Belovèd's family would not have it.

'Is there something wrong with the footsteps of the sister?' asked the doctor, hanging his stethoscope around his neck.

'No, no, there's nothing wrong; but if Belovèd had walked down such a path she'd surely have lost herself.'

Suddenly the tall man remembered something. He remarked animatedly, 'There's an elderly woman among Belovèd's elders. That woman's household members show her much respect but they never allow her to leave the house. I've heard that the strong old lady has grown weak from imprisonment. Her relations greet her respectfully, but no one will sit by her for long.'

All at once the voice of someone demanding dal and rice came from behind the curtain. It was a sweet, feminine voice. After a short while, that same voice began to recount the tale of Ram, Sita, Lanka, and Hanuman.

The doctor glanced in surprise at the tall man as though he couldn't believe his ears, but the tall man's sober gaze reassured him. The doctor looked back at the patient. Her condition remained unchanged.

'You were saying that as evening falls, a fresh breeze comes through the window of the room next door?'

'Yes! Though the breeze arrives in the evening, its fresh air gladdens the heart like the morning breezes of the Zephyr. Has evening already fallen?' he suddenly asked agitatedly.

'No, there's still a bit of time left. Do you have no sense of the passage of time?' The tall man remained silent. There was something about that question that made him even more anxious.

The doctor stared at him questioningly. He turned a needle-sharp gaze on the tall man, and finally he replied in a deep and helpless voice, 'No.'

'That is very surprising.' The doctor could think of nothing else to say.

But he continued to stare at the tall man, who could not withstand his gaze. Very softly he spoke:

'For many days now, I have felt as though all times of the day were sunset.'

'Are you closed up inside the walls of the house at all times as well?' the doctor asked searchingly.

This time the man responded with grim silence, which frightened the doctor.

The man guessed at the doctor's reaction. He spoke in a cheerful tone:

'Many things are mysterious, and it could be that even if I were to pull the curtain away from the secret, you would still be unable to understand.'

The two of them were silent for a long time. Then the doctor took the lead.

'All I want to know is, when a fresh breeze enters the room, what sort of change comes to the patient's condition?'

'Why don't you see for yourself when evening falls?'

'There's still some time until then.'

The two of them again fell silent. The doctor felt as though no one else was especially interested in the woman's life besides the tall man. He hadn't seen the women asking after the patient's health, but he could certainly tell that they were only taking an interest in her health in the manner that people ask one another about changes in the weather. What he couldn't understand was what importance this awe-inspiring man held in this community. What connection did he have to the other inhabitants of the building and what is the connection between the man and the sprawling settlement outside. All sorts of questions came to his mind, but due to the seriousness of the man's tone and the apparent delicacy of the situation, he didn't feel like asking too many of them.

He tried a roundabout question, and asked, 'Whose locality is this outside?'

'Have you come here for the first time?'

'Yes, I'd only seen it from a distance. I like the way it looks. The height of these buildings, their strength and age, attract the eye from a distance. Today I saw the bazaar from up close as well: the colourful wares, assorted types of clothing, the many ethnicities of the people, and then the cries of all the sadhus and holy men. I didn't have a chance to see much. But when I saw the old-style bricks of the outside building, I felt a great sense of peace that such simplicity could exist in this community as well.'

'Come, let me show you something of the community. When sunset draws near, please do tell me. Then we'll come back to the patient.'

He opened the high dark teak doors, and the two of them left the room. They encountered many types of people in the corridor, but no one addressed them. The doctor felt that even though no one addressed them, everyone viewed the imposing, handsome, and well-dressed man with veneration and love. This section of the corridor was across from a wide stairway. The two of them walked up the stairs, and kept climbing higher and higher, passing the rooftop terraces of countless buildings, until they reached the highest rooftop of all. This rooftop was bounded by crested battlements. The man grabbed his hand and led him to stand by the edge of these. The entire settlement was sprawled out below them. The yellow rays of the sun still fell upon the roof, but below, far below, darkness had already fallen in the bazaars.

The doctor had the sensation that even though darkness had fallen, the bazaars below still bustled with activity. This made him realise that this exuberant activity came not from sunlight but from the community itself. The tall, strong building on which they stood was surrounded by bazaars on all sides and the brick building that adjoined it; these were all cloaked in a silken darkness from which he could still hear the hubbub of voices.

'To whom does all this belong?' he asked as he gazed below at the settlement.

'These buildings, these pillars, these balconies, these battlements, these bazaars and clamorous voices, all belong to me, and emanate from me alone,' the man replied earnestly.

Some shadowy figures clad in white appeared below, in the simple brick building; their facial features were indistinct due to the smudged darkness.

'And who are those people?' asked the doctor impetuously.

The man gazed down at the figures respectfully and said after a pause:

'That building and those white-clad persons causing the commotion are all part of this settlement as well. All the individuals in the bazaar are also part of the community. All the inhabitants of this building are a part of it too, and all have become fragmented due to the illness of the patient.'

'What do you mean?' The doctor's eyes widened.

'All their lives are deeply connected to this woman. On a conscious level none of them even realise how critical she was to their existence, but since she's fallen ill, since she's grown weak, everyone is finding their lives diminished in some way or the other.'

'Your words are like riddles,' the doctor said in a hushed tone. Now he felt fearful, though he was beginning to understand a bit more. As the last rays of the sun disappeared into darkness, he stood by the battlements of the broad roof of that illustrious building towering above the sprawling settlement below, and found himself awe-struck. But now he could no longer hold back his questions.

'But who is the patient? You haven't told me that yet. You've not yet told me anything about your connection to her,' the doctor finally found the courage to ask the question on his mind, up there in the open air of the roof.

The man continued to peer below the battlements. Suddenly he spoke: 'You were able to understand nothing yourself?' His questioning eyes were filled with sadness.

Then it was that the doctor felt as though a sort of curtain had been pulled aside. He recalled that when he had listened to the beating of the patient's heart, he'd also heard some voices that he'd often heard before and been gladdened by.

He looked carefully at the tall, handsome man, then stood with his head bowed.

'Evening has fallen. Come, let's go downstairs and take a look at the patient.'

The two of them rushed quickly down the stairs. The moment they entered the door, they could feel the fresh gusts of air blowing in from the next room. The patient was sitting up on the bed, leaning against the bolster with dignity; her face had turned a rosy pink. When she saw the doctor enter, she stood on no formalities, but when her eyes rested on the tall man, they filled with gratitude.

'How are you?' the tall man asked softly in tones of marvellous love as he drew near.

She smiled with difficulty, and gazed at the man with big round eyes as she spoke respectfully:

'I always get well at this time.'

'Doctor Sahib says that your vital signs are for the most part healthy. You just have a shortage of fresh air to breathe in.'

The patient sat silently, her head down.

'But why do you get so upset?' she asked after a while.

'You know that the business of living in this settlement was established because of me. If, God forbid, you were to perish, then everything would slowly turn to straw and scatter to the four winds.'

'But,' the doctor stopped him to ask, 'can it not be that the window in the next room remain always open and fresh air always blow in?'

'In the next rooms there are other inhabitants, among them some young men. In all the rooms on all sides there is only one room where the inhabitant has opened the window. When he returns in the evening he opens this door. Only then can the breeze enter. He runs around all day earning his daily bread. He is only able to come home at evening's fall.'

'Can't the rest of the people open the windows of their dwellings as well as their doors on this side?' the doctor asked.

'Perhaps they no longer have any interest in this woman now.'

'Then why is this young man interested?'

'Because he wants to see her alive.'

'Why is that?'

'Because he loves his ancestors.'

'I do not understand what you mean,' said the doctor hopelessly.

'I had mentioned before that even if I tried to explain, you wouldn't necessarily comprehend,' the man replied in a morose tone.

'Then is there nothing I can do?' asked the doctor as though laying down his weapons in surrender.

'You are a doctor. You'd be best able to tell us what you can do.'

'I can only give medicine for strengthening the lungs, but the true medicine for such a condition is fresh air.' The doctor spoke firmly but respectfully. After staying in this environment for so long, he was finally able to speak clearly and precisely. Then he spoke again, 'Tell all the young male inhabitants of this building to open all their outward facing windows as well as the doors that open into this room.'

'But if they won't, then ... then ... what will happen?' asked the patient impulsively.

'Then ...' said the doctor, emphasising each and every word, '... then he will be finished.' He motioned towards the tall, handsome man.

No one was there to witness the glances exchanged by the lovely sad patient and the tall handsome man, for the doctor, shielding his gaze from both, had quietly picked up his bag and snuck outside.

—*Translated by Daisy Rockwell*

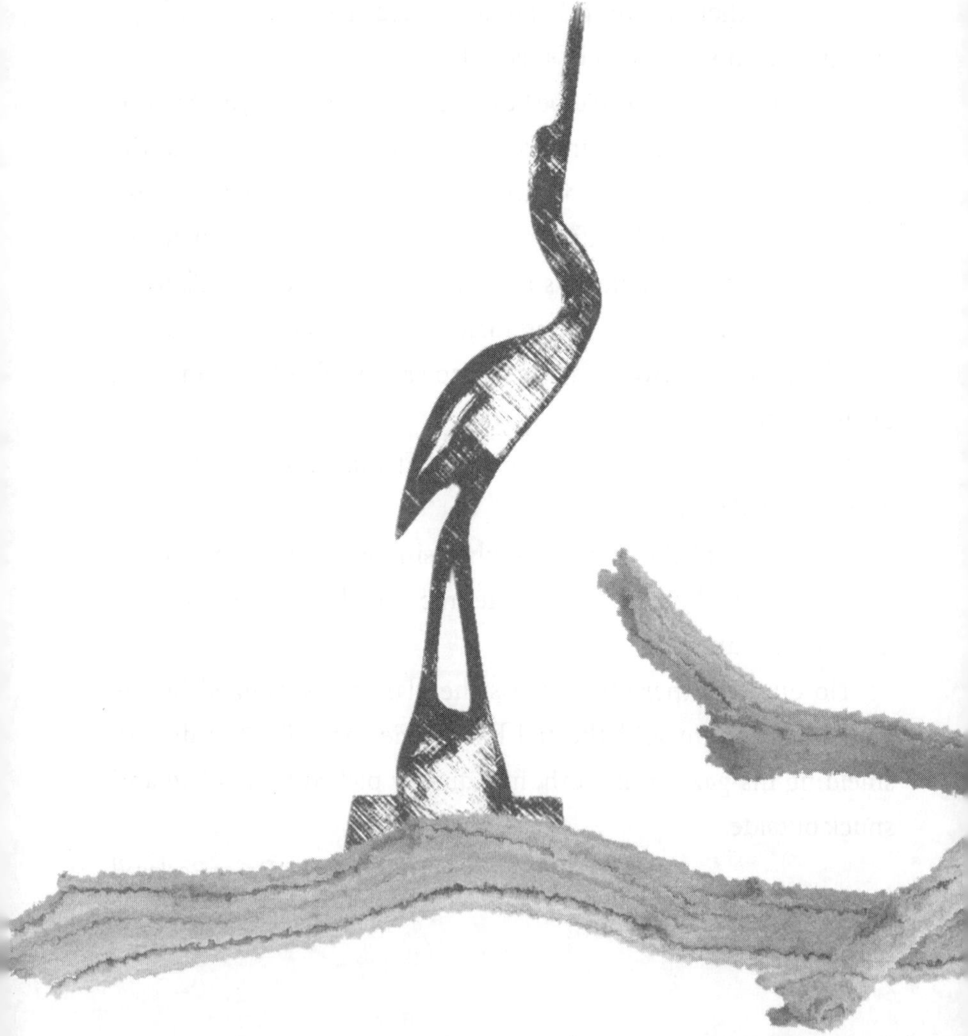

Driftwood

Deepak Budki

This dates back to the days when I used to serve in the Army. I had a friend, Colonel Kaul. He was very fond of collecting bits of driftwood ... driftwood, or dried up, lifeless twigs that had fallen from trees in storms and then got carried away by forceful winds.

The decrepit pieces of wood that, if not salvaged by Colonel Kaul, would have been consigned to the home-fires of some poor labourer. Colonel Kaul would not pick up just any piece of wood that he would find to adorn his drawing room. He preferred small, durable and strong branches. How painstakingly and skilfully he carved those broken fragments of branches, peeled off their barks! And then sand-papered them to a smooth finish and finally applied varnish to transform them into artistic masterpieces.

Our Army Division was exploring the banks of the river Brahmaputra and bringing this remote, uninhabited area to life for a short while. Our tents had been pitched beside the river. Due to constant rains, the ground was covered with dense vegetation. One day, the Colonel and I ventured out for a walk by the riverbank when he suddenly stopped and turned around. On a sandy stretch he spotted a piece of wood. He quickly sprinted towards it and pounced upon it as if it were a treasure. He then proceeded to continue walking with the piece of wood in his hand. He had the gleeful look of a diver, who emerges from the water, with a rare pearl. He turned to me and said, 'Colonel Sapru, see what a beauty it is! See how much natural beauty there is in this piece of wood. Look at this ... a crane's beak, its two long legs, its arched neck, its splayed wings ... Have you ever been to the Bharatpur Bird Sanctuary? Peace be upon the soul of Dr Salim Ali ... I saw a crane just like this there.'

A few days later, I visited the Colonel in his tent. I was surprised to see the driftwood. It actually seemed transformed into a beautiful crane. As I returned to my tent, I thought about the most important driftwood adorning the Colonel's tent. That driftwood, which was uprooted and then battered by strong winds and then lay scattered on the cold, wet sands, awaiting its fate.

Colonel Kaul was no stranger to me. We both hailed from the same city, had gone to the same school, had secured admission in the NDA in the same year and were allotted the same training unit. In other words, we had practically lived our lives close to one another. As we finished our work beside the riverbank, we headed back to the Guwahati Cantonment where our families awaited us.

A few days later, I visited Colonel Kaul at his home, along with my wife. In the drawing room, I saw the carved driftwood creation displayed proudly on a corner table. Mrs Kaul, who excelled at Ikebana, had placed an exquisite floral display next to it that enhanced its beauty even more. My wife went to the kitchen to join Mrs Kaul for a chat. Colonel Kaul got up to open his wine cabinet and poured scotch into two glasses. Just then, I had the opportunity to inspect the driftwood that Colonel Kaul had picked up from the riverside with me, more closely. Alongside the Ikebana arrangement, there was also a photograph of the Colonel's only child — his daughter Suman.

Seeing her photograph, I took my glass from Colonel Kaul and asked, 'Any news of Suman?'

'Yes, she is in Dubai these days,' he said, as he took a sip of whiskey.

'How is she?'

'She's fine. She is working as a private secretary in a company these days. She gets paid handsomely. Every month she sends us something.'

'Oh you are a lucky guy! These days children do not care about their parents at all,' I said by way of reassurance.

We reached home around 10:00 pm. My wife fell asleep as soon as she lay down but sleep evaded me. Suman's entire life played out in my mind, like scenes from a film. Since her childhood, whenever she would be in any kind of turmoil, she would tiptoe up to my wife and confide in her. So I was perfectly well aware of all that happened in her life.

After a long wait of five years, when Suman was born, the house was awash with happiness. Colonel Kaul had taken quite a while to settle down and then had to endure an extra delay of five years. Poor Mrs Kaul, who was a few years older than her husband, was relieved to have finally borne a child.

So fearful was she of her own precarious position in her marriage that she never questioned her husband on any issue. She remained blind to everything that happened right in front of her eyes and simply tolerated everything as she believed it was a wife's duty to keep her husband happy at all times. How much he drank, how many cigarettes he smoked, what company he kept or whether he fulfilled her basic conjugal needs, were of no especial concern to her. After all, Eastern women tend not to get involved too much in these issues in any case.

A discernible change was seen in Colonel Kaul after his daughter's birth. He began to take a keen interest in her upbringing. The food she ate, the clothes she wore, the school she attended, everything was decided solely by Colonel Kaul. He secured her admission at St Peter's School where, as time went by, she grew up into a young lady.

Since childhood, Suman had the unfortunate habit of sucking her thumb and this stayed with her even as she grew up. Her mother made many attempts to get her to stop but each time she reprimanded her daughter, Colonel Kaul would step in and brush it aside. The mother worried about being able to find a suitable groom for her daughter due to this bad habit. Mothers tend to start worrying about their daughter's marriage from the time they give birth to them.

But Mrs Kaul did not pay any attention to another development that she should have. Since childhood Suman slept in her father's bed and would not give up this habit. The only difference was that Mrs Kaul found this habit inconsequential whereas the thumb-sucking was, for her, socially unacceptable.

Suman would cling tightly to her father and sleep. In the cold mountainous climate, bodily warmth is a godsend but as her body began to change, this closeness took a very different turn. Colonel Kaul got drunk every night on a regular basis. His temper increasingly became volatile. On a nightly basis, his hands would wander freely along Suman's body. And as time went by, these nocturnal explorations crossed the limits of propriety. On the one hand, Suman's awareness and senses had become far more acute and on the other there was a sense of personal loss and great restlessness of mind to experience all that she was experiencing at such a young age.

It had a strange effect on Suman. In such situations, girls generally tend to harbour feelings of self-loathing and disgust and are plunged into depression. But Suman cloaked her sadness with peals of laughter. She attempted to assuage her broken and damaged inner being with physical intimacy and proceeded by using men to smoothen her way through life.

She seemed to blossom the moment she entered the gates of College. She exuded charm and allure. Wherever she went, she bedazzled those around her. Her cheerful appearance gave no indication of any trouble in her life. A smile on her lips remained in place all the time, like a coating of lipstick. Kashmiri girls tend to be very fair in complexion but in her case her colour would put even alabaster to shame. Soon, she took on numerous lovers. Some in quick succession, some concurrently. She counted them, like a child would count her toys, play with them for a few days and then toss them away when she grew tired of them. She seemed to be taking revenge on life in her own way.

Going to Mumbai and launching her modelling career was her greatest desire. This wish tugged at her heart most keenly when she sat in front of her mirror stroking her long, lustrous hair. Colonel Kaul, however, wanted her to become either a doctor or an engineer. As it so happened, she became neither a doctor nor an engineer; nor was there any progress in her Mumbai plans.

But Suman was not one to be dejected by minor setbacks. She had, over the years, mastered the art of extracting nectar from flowers, like butterflies do. She did not want to be tied down to any lasting situation. She was adept at manipulating her friends and parents. The experiences of her life had taught her a valuable lesson: that her beauty and youth were her greatest treasures and she wanted to prolong her days of youth as much as possible.

The prospect of becoming a model prompted Suman to plan another strategy. Her parents were keen to see her married off. One day she stood in front of her parents with Abhay to seek their blessing. She wore *sindoor* in the parting of her hair and had got her marriage registered in court. Colonel Kaul did not seem too concerned with this development. What could he do? What right did he have to influence her decisions? He sported a fake smile and attempted to welcome his son-in-law, drinking his disappointment along with gulps of whiskey. Abhay reciprocated his attempts. In the kitchen, her mother wept silent tears as she fried *pakodas*.

Within a month, news came from Mumbai that Suman and Abhay had fought. They had filed for divorce proceedings. Suman knocked on various doors, looking for modelling assignments. But apart from small insignificant jobs, she never got her big break. She entertained many and slept with numerous promoters but success eluded her. Her childhood dream of taking part in a beauty contest too faded in a few months. She met a model from Kerala at the advertising company she worked at and started sharing a room with her.

Almost a year went by. Suman was not at all content with her lot. She felt rebellious and restless again. In this past year Suman had come to realise the bitter truths of life. She now knew the value of wealth and wanted to escape the wretchedness of her life in Mumbai. She was unable to find any release even though her divorce had come through by now.

It was the month of November. Diwali was two days away. Suman sat in her room on a chair with her legs perched on a table, drinking tea.

She was bored of her loneliness. Just then her friend Elizabeth, whom she fondly called Liz, entered the room and exclaimed, 'I have a surprise for you, man!'

Liz came over with two letters and kissed her on the lips. Suman's eyes sparkled as Liz handed her an envelope. 'It's a Diwali card. From your father. The only man you love in this world,' Liz sounded playful. Suman had confided in her friend.

Suman opened the card and looked at it, kissing it many times.

'Dad you are simply great. I was waiting for so long. My day is made! I love you dad ... I love you!'

As Suman continued to gaze at the card, Liz had opened and read the second letter.

'Sweetheart!'

Suman looked at her questioningly.

'My sister Ruby has written from Dubai ... she works at a famous hospital as a nurse. She is on very good terms with the owner of the hospital. We might get a well-deserved break. Touchwood!

Suman quickly touched the wooden table under her feet.

'Darling, the owner of the hospital, Sheikh Abdullah Al Kabir Al Mustafa owns a large retail chain. He has supermarkets in different cities of UAE. He is about to launch a campaign for which he needs Indian models. He is coming to Mumbai on Sunday. My sister has given him my contact .What a great surprise Sumi! I suggest we go and welcome him at the airport. You know the Arab psyche. He will take one look and ...' Liz left the rest unsaid.

Abdullah's eyes were bedazzled by Suman's beauty when he met her at the airport. He had no inkling that two gorgeous girls would be waiting for him. Over the next few days he wrapped up his work and planned to leave for Dubai.

On his last night, he invited both Suman and Liz for dinner at the Taj Mahal Hotel. He sat across from Suman and addressed her, 'Miss Suman, I have an offer for you.'

'What is it?' Suman smiled.

'Miss Suman, why don't you come to Dubai?'

Suman and Liz looked at one another with a puzzled expression. Despite her best efforts, Suman was finding it difficult to conceal her glee.

Abdullah said he would appoint her as a private secretary with a salary of 1.5 thousand dollars.

For a moment, Suman closed her eyes. She could not believe this was happening in reality and not just in a dream. In her mind, the image of her success rose dimming the sense of rejection in the beauty contest. Her face had lined discernibly with age and the turmoil of life though she tried to conceal it with layers of makeup.

Liz signalled with her eyes, 'Say yes'.

'It is alright. My passport is ready. You arrange for my visa,' Suman assented as she met Abdullah's eyes.

The visa was arranged and Suman left for Dubai. She informed her father as soon as she reached Dubai. Later that night, she chatted with her parents on the phone for a long time. Colonel Kaul kept receiving numerous emails and detailed letters from her. She kept him abreast of all the developments in Mumbai and Dubai. At the end of each letter she always wrote, 'I love you dad ... I love you!'

She would tell him in great detail about her day-to-day life in Dubai. She never concealed any aspect of her life from her father except for the fact that she was now gracing the harem of Sheikh Abdullah Al Kabir Al Mustafa.

—Translated by Tabinda Burney

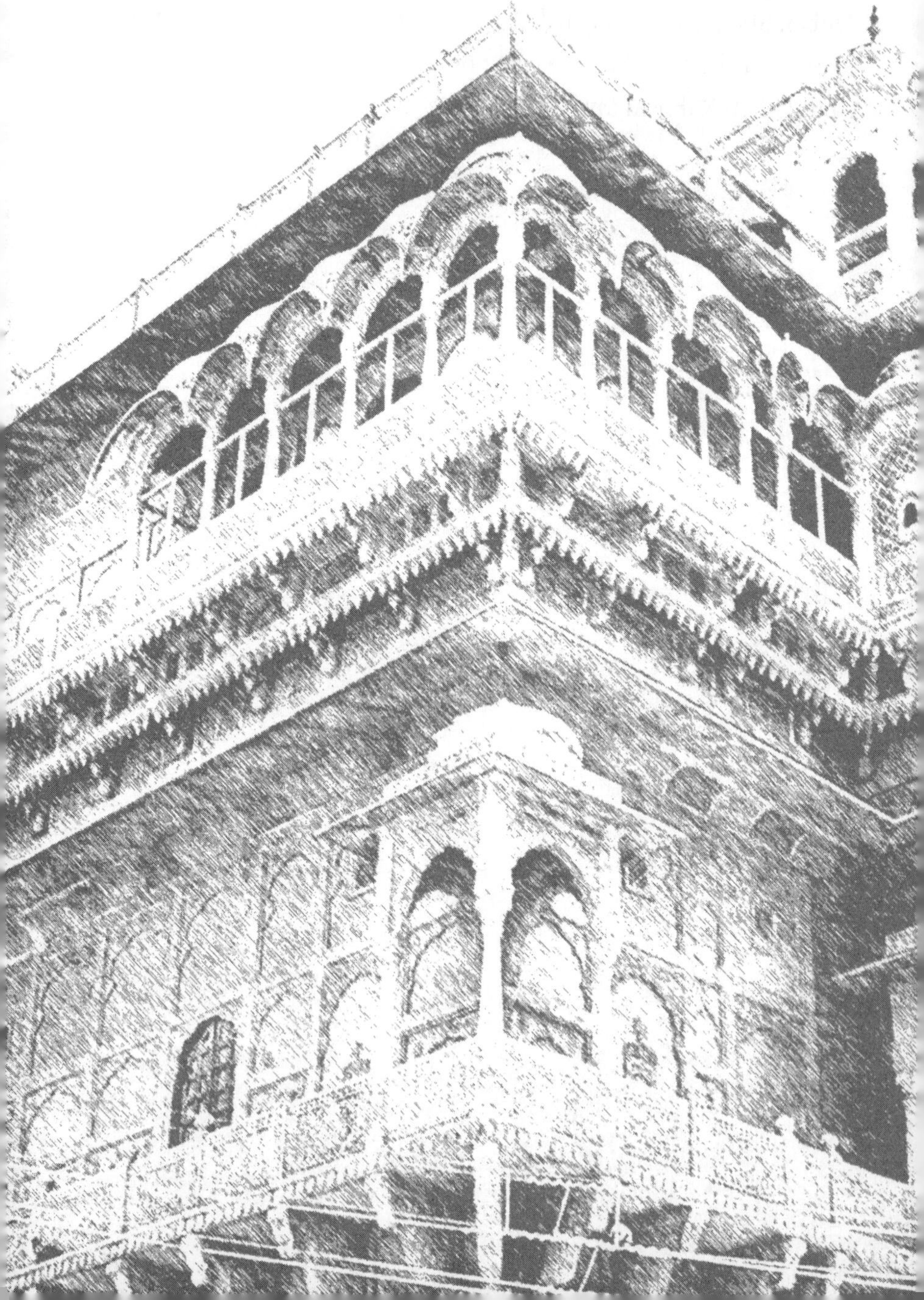

The Unexpected Disaster

Hussainul Haque

Bibi Izzat-un Nisa was busy winding up her daily tasks as quickly as she could. When she leaned out of the kitchen window and glanced around, she realised that the evening was drawing closer but her chores didn't seem to end. An afternoon siesta had turned her schedule upside down. After she was done with the utensils, she remembered the pile of clothes, full of filth and faecal matter that needed to be washed.

With the children growing older, she had thought that she would be relieved of this laundry routine at least, but who can alter the misfortunes destined to befall us! Her husband had been struck with paralysis and was bedridden. All he could utter was 'food' and 'water' that too with much effort. Any minor ailment could turn a man's temper into an irritable state, and Izzat-un Nisa's husband's ailment was a serious one. While he was hale and hearty, keeping up to his name, he never let anything or anyone take him for granted. There was absolutely no chance of him tolerating anything outside his comfort zone and nobody could dare solve an issue without consulting him — at home or in the neighbourhood. From perverse to debased language, to abuses, he could go to any length to pamper his ego.

Izzat-un Nisa was taken aback by this bestial demeanour when she got married and came to live with her in-laws. But her sisters-in-law, her friends and relatives all advised her to ignore his behaviour for a while as it was typical of the landlord culture he belonged to. He was the proverbial *spoilt nawab* of an influential family, they said. With perseverance and generous caring, she would be able to imprison him slowly in her love. His sharp tongue and authoritarian ways could be tamed according to her will, they advised.

Following these suggestions Bibi Izzat-un Nisa, started experimenting with her affection. She believed that her usual meticulous and impeccable mannerisms alone would not suffice if she had to gain his attention and kindness. But Jalal-uddin had this hidden monster inside him that, leave alone the usual times, would emerge even at the time of lovemaking. His use of brutal force made the act of making love utterly bestial. Whenever she would be in the mood for tenderness, he would find an excuse to pick a fight with her that would conclude in slaps and violence, after which he would turn away and drift into a peaceful slumber. Izzat-un Nisa dared not to melt his mood to entice him. By the time Jalal-uddin would tame his boorish ways to some extent and get drawn to her, it would be time for her menstruation and she would expect some relief in this period. But those few days were the most terrible ones. Every month, during that week, he would pinch and assault her not just in his usual bestial ways but with all the characteristics of a mad man and the entire exercise would be nothing but pure torment. She would try to escape the ordeal but she couldn't and to add to it during those days there would be a river of desire flowing upward within her. Despite all the violence, the meeting of two bodies would ultimately result in heightened emotions. Despite her tired body, and blinded by the emotional turmoil, she would quietly lie down with her eyes closed and let the tornado take over her senses.

The Unexpected Disaster: Hussainul Haque

All three of her children were beautiful reminders, conceived in and around those cruel days.

This continued for about seven or eight years of their marriage till her husband had a paralytic stroke. Doctors ascribed it to high blood pressure. Izzat-un Nisa wasn't surprised. It wasn't difficult to figure out the cause of such high blood pressure. It was a natural fallout given Jalal-uddin's nature. But the cause of his high pressure did not take its toll on him alone; it managed to cripple the entire household.

It wasn't just Jalal-uddin's anger that was sustained by the lands he owned, but the sustenance of the entire household depended on the revenue from those lands. All acquaintances vanished over time along with the landlord's power. His brothers too shifted to other cities when the lands were taken away. Later came the news that they had migrated to Pakistan. The only people left in his family were his parents, who unable to bear this fury of fate, departed from this world one after the other within a year. Her family too had earlier left for Pakistan. Her entire universe now centred around her three children and a paralytic husband.

Life for her had become a lacerated wound in the head of a dog already suffering from rabid scabies.

It was during one of these days that Lala Harihar Prasad visited her house.

Lala Harihar Prasad was the younger brother of Jalal-uddin's family accountant, Munshi Lala Bansidhar Prasad. Bansidhar was the same age as Jalal-uddin but would never sit down before or beside Jalal-uddin. He would resemble a dog wagging his tail whenever he climbed the steps of the haveli. He would take off his shoes the moment he entered the house, adjust his dhoti and sit down on the bench placed in the outside verandah. He would keep sitting there calmly even if nobody showed up for an hour or so. When somebody from the house would step out and see him sitting on the bench, he would ask them to inform the master about his arrival. But in spite of that there was no guarantee that Jalal-uddin would acknowledge Lala's presence and meet him.

His job was to sit and wait. And leave only when Jalal-uddin allowed it.

All the household necessities, from groceries to jewellery, were managed by Lala alone. Nobody gave him any money, nor did he ever ask for it. Jalal-uddin himself never asked for accounts of the income or expenditure from Lala. All the issues related to the farm, the land given for agriculture/tenancy, Lala tended himself. Every deposit and withdrawal, buying and selling of land, were handled by Bansidhar. After all, he was in charge of all finances.

But when the landlord culture came to an end, what task could be assigned to Lala?

That orchard would have definitely been left intact. But who could she ask? Jalal-uddin was beyond that ability of asking or replying. Living corpses were never in a position to ask questions or answer queries. She could have asked Lala Bansidhar, but where was he to be found? Lala, who would be in attendance at the haveli everyday, had not visited them once in the last 5-6 months. Earlier, at the onset of Jalal-uddin's paralysis, he visited them regularly for about two months or so. But once he had gathered from the doctors that the paralysis would stay with Jalal-uddin till his demise and that he was not in a position to share any details with anybody whosoever, Lala's daily visits dwindled to a routine absence.

The Unexpected Disaster: Hussainul Haque

When Lala's absence was finally established and the household stuff started to be sold to fulfil the day to day needs, then....

For the first time Izzat-un Nisa crossed the threshold of her haveli.

Putting on her veil, and wearing her burqa, she reached the front gate. Immediately the family's traditional palanquin bearer Ghooran came to her.

'Malkin, are you planning to go somewhere?'

'I am thinking of going to Lala Bansidhar's house.'

'Why are you going there? I will go and call him.'

She gave a cynical laugh, 'Those times are long gone by. Now I *will have* to go ...'

'Okay, if that be your wish. Please stay here, I will bring the doli.'

'Don't bother, I will walk down.'

Ghooran started pleading in an emotionally charged voice, 'Till I am alive, this cannot be.'

She laughed with a hint of authority, 'All right, go and get the doli.'

There was an instant buzz in Lala Bansidhar's house when Izzat-un Nisa arrived. Ghooran had announced, the moment they reached,

'The doli has come from the malkin's house.'

Lala's old mother immediately came outside the front door to greet her, stunned at her sudden appearance.

'Malkin, you came here yourself?'

'Yes mataji, I thought I should visit you.' She answered with a smile while her eyes swept over the house.

Their accountant's haveli was bigger than theirs.

It was surrounded by huge and magnificent fort-like walls. One part was cordoned off for the servant's quarters, a stable stood on the other side and a cow shed occupied the third corner. There was a small temple on the side adjacent to the well and Lala's haveli towered in the centre. There was an outhouse and an inner space. Stretching through the expanse and connecting the two was a small courtyard. Through the same courtyard, mataji took her inside the house.

All the family members were there except Lala Bansidhar!

The first person she saw was Lala Harihar Prasad.

He was undoubtedly handsome: with a clear fair complexion, sharp features and average height. He was impressive at the first glance. Immediately a thought crossed her mind, 'He is younger than Bansidhar, might be a year or two older than me.'

She had not crossed thirty-two yet.

After some polite small talk, she came to the point, 'Mataji, where is Lala Bansidhar?'

'Don't ask me his whereabouts, I have borne him but he has turned into a stranger, one we could never have imagined. Three months ago he went to Delhi with his wife and children. Had Harihar not been with us, we would have been devastated by now.'

'Any idea of his whereabouts there?' Izzat-un Nisa felt her voice drowning in a sea of hopelessness.

'None at all Bibi. The only thing he said before leaving was that he doesn't want to stay in this city anymore. We know nothing besides that.'

Izzat-un Nisa could see that mataji did not want to talk about Bansidhar.

She also understood the underlying implications of this knowledge on her fate and this very fact made her heart sink.

'Okay mataji, I will take your leave now.'

She cried to her heart's content all the way back home.

She was lost in a reverie of times gone by. Her childhood days, the courtyard of her parental home, the flowers and fruits in her backyard garden, friends and relatives, all those games she played as a child, a distant cousin who would stare at her at every opportunity and she would run away giggling at his crazy absurdity. Bibi lived through many decades as she sat in the doli that day.

She found her home in utter chaos when she got back.

Her husband had soiled the bed and the children were crying. Her elder daughter was trying her level best to handle the mess but her father was not easy to handle with such utter confusion all around. Izzat-un Nisa first cleaned up her husband, then tended to the children and then turned her attention to the kitchen. It was dark by the time she finished all her chores. When she finally hit the bed after feeding everyone, her senses were in disarray. She could not think of any consoling balm that could be applied in these circumstances. Leave alone her husband's treatment, even arranging for food and clothes would be a challenge. She racked her brains but could not think of anybody who could come to her rescue in these turbulent times. There was this utter mayhem of 1947, and then the second one was after the abolition of zamindari system, all those near and dear ones on whom she could have depended upon to ease her towering burdens, had migrated to Pakistan. Had this tragedy not befallen Jalal-uddin, a tragedy which rendered him disabled for the rest of his life, they too would have shifted to Pakistan.

In the six months that followed, life took on a completely different track. The golden era of abundance and prosperity under the zamindari system had come to an end. Household stuff got sold. Her stature altered from malkin to a tutor. When this too proved to be insufficient, she started stitching clothes for children and reading *milaad* in people's homes. But with the mammoth task of living, all these possibilities were not showing any silver lining worth a try that would elevate her days to some relaxed moments. The local doctor had advised her to give the juice of pigeon's meat to her husband; Maulvi Sahab's fees were yet to be paid. The new academic year had begun and the issue of buying new course books for the children was adding to her pile of woes. While she could somehow manage to alleviate the day-to-day issues, the matters looming in the future filled her with dread. She sometimes felt as if her head would burst.

It was during these testing times that Lala Harihar Prasad visited her house.

The month of *Shabaan* was almost near its end and it was the last stages of the moon too. Darkness was pouring in like cloudbursts on the haveli. The fog had enveloped the entire neighbourhood even though the night hadn't yet descended. The door had not been latched yet. Suddenly she sensed someone was standing at the threshold.

Izzat-un Nisa couldn't imagine who could have come at this hour on a cold and dark night such as this? She raised the wick of the dim lantern and moved towards the front door with her daughter Ruqayya.

She could see a silhouette in the light of the lantern she was carrying. Lala Hari Prasad was standing at the door....'

'Lalaji?'

Lala Hari Prasad stood there with folded hands.

For a while she kept looking at him, unable to figure out what she should do. But in a flash she regained her composure.

'Please wait a moment Lalaji,' saying so she quickly dashed in and opened the door of the sitting room. She swiftly dusted the two chairs and table, the only furniture that remained, and leapt towards the door. 'Lalaji please come in!'

Lalaji entered the sitting room with slow and reluctant steps. When she asked him to sit down, Lalaji folded his hands and pleaded, 'Excuse me, I cannot sit unless you do so.'

She sat down with a smile.

All humility, Lalaji sat down tentatively, sitting on the edge of the chair, as if on tenterhooks. .

A desert of silence stretched between them for some time. Izzat-un Nisa felt that Lala was hesitant to initiate the conversation.

'What brings you here today?'

'I am most embarrassed,' he folded his hands again. 'I wanted to come earlier but somehow couldn't gather the courage. Today I was passing by here and felt a strange compulsion.'

Izzat-un Nisa looked at him with a bemused expression and listened to him with studied attention. There was a strange mixture of hesitation and confusion in Lala's voice. She remembered her distant cousin who was crazily in love with her. He met her once after she got married and asked in a very dull voice, 'How are you? My eyes have been deprived of your sight.' Later, whenever his voice reverberated in her mind, she felt as if a dying man was saying his last goodbye. And she shuddered.

It was uncanny that Lalaji's voice reminded her of that love-crazed young man from her past.

That day Lala stayed for a very short time. He made some small talk and left. One day ... two days ... four days and when the entire week passed, Izzat-un Nisa had forgotten about his visit. As usual her days passed by, purposeless and hopeless.

And then, on one of those idle and empty days, Lala Harihar Prasad came on a second visit. He enquired about the children as soon as he sat down.

'They have slept,' Izzat-un Nisa quietly answered.

'Ruqayya?'

'No, she is studying.'

'Would you please call her?'

Izzat-un Nisa went inside and called Ruqayya to the sitting room. Lala touched her chin and kissed her. He caressed her head and gave her a packet that he had brought with him, 'This is for you and your siblings.'

Ruqayya's hand unconsciously moved towards the packet, but suddenly stopped. She looked at her mother's eyes.

'What's the need for all this Lalaji?'

Lala simply folded his hands.

'This is for the children. I came across a sweet shop on my way here and thought they would enjoy them.'

'Take it, Ruqayya, it's rude to not accept presents.' Her eyes dimmed with tears as she said this, as she tried to recall the last time her children had a sweet treat, but her memory refused to come to her aid.

'Get some tea,' Izzat-un Nisa said in a soft voice when Ruqayya was about to leave.

The Unexpected Disaster: Hussainul Haque

'It's quite late now, please don't bother.' Lalaji spoke and his hands folded, yet again.

'Lala, this was the time the merry-making started in the haveli once upon a time.' Izzat-un Nisa could not hide the soft lament in her voice.

From that moment, Izzat-un Nisa started opening up to Lala. He would visit every alternate day and would bring something or the other for the children.

Then one day Lala came, sat for a while and got up to leave early. He stopped at the exit door just before leaving, turned towards Izzat-un Nisa and gave her a handkerchief pressed between his palms. His demeanour at this moment was extremely humble and his voice had a pleading and fearful tone, 'Please don't refuse this.'

Izzat-un Nisa could not discern anything. Dark night. Sharp breeze, the chaotic emotions.... How could I protect the candle in the wind? How can someone as weak as me stay upright in these storms?

Before she could decide what to do, Lala pressed the handkerchief in her hands and stepped out.

Izzat-un Nisa closed the door behind her and stood leaning against it. She opened the handkerchief. It was the night of the new moon and she peered at the small bundle in her hand. There were five notes of hundred rupees tied neatly into the handkerchief. She sat there at the door and cried her heart out.

Lala did not come for another ten or fifteen days. This period proved to be a kind of testing period. The house was at its peak of utter chaos. The money tied up in that hanky was lying at the bottom of her trunk, waiting for the warmth of a touch. During those times, the children cried several times, she herself broke down umpteen number of times. Exasperated, she felt overwhelmed as the realisation hit her that there was nobody to enquire about her welfare. In one such desultory moment, she looked at her husband and found herself in the grip of mixed emotions — anger, hatred, sympathy all at the same time.

In those exhausting moments, the question which consumed her was, 'This man was being punished for his deeds, fine. What was the indiscretion for which she and her children were suffering?' It was beyond her comprehension.

Sometimes she would get tired of the daily rigmarole and start mentally exploring possibilities. She would think, 'It is impossible that Lala Harihar is unaware of Bansidhar's financial control on my household and he certainly must be familiar with all the transactions regarding my husband's assets. It is possible that Harihar would have informed Lala Bansidhar and he would have sent the money.' She would run towards the trunk with these convincing thoughts in her head. But, as she would unlock it, she would again get into confused. 'Mataji had made it very clear that they have no idea of Bansidhar's whereabouts. They don't even have his address to send letters to. Then where could this money have come from?' she would suddenly stop, shake her head, wipe her tears and walk away from the trunk.

Life is made up of myriad shades of colours and moods, spring takes over autumn, humidity over fresh breeze...!

Izzat-un Nisa's life was akin to somebody trapped in a whirling tornado.

'But where is the rapture, Izzat-un Nisa?'

In one of those penetratingly crushing moments, Lala Hari Prasad knocked on the door.

After some light conversation, Izzat-un Nisa asked, 'Did you receive any letter from Lala Bansidhar?'

'No, I don't know anything of him.'

'And don't you plan to look for him?'

'I wanted to, but mataji did not let me.'

'Why does she not want to know about him?'

'Please let's leave it here, I don't want to go into the details.'

'But, Lala ... this detail is essential to my survival. Please don't hide anything.'

Harihar relaxed and answered in a dull voice, 'He had a fight with mataji. She advised him to return all the remaining property of which he is the guardian, to the real owners.'

What was left to ask now? She understood all that Lala was trying to hide and even Lala knew her concerns and questions.

There was some kind of supernatural transmission. The dark night, hurtling down the corridor with slow but deliberate speed, was busy forming a network of strong emotions. Izzat-un Nisa wanted to break this network, but she felt trapped in a labyrinth. Suddenly her house seemed to be suffering a paralytic stroke.

She felt she may have been a woman, at some point of time. But right now, she was a housefly who some demon had pinned to a wall.

She looked at Lala Hariprasad penetratingly.

Was he that demon?

Hariprasad's face was angelic, pure and innocent. Suddenly he got to his feet and said, 'I will take your leave now.'

'Lalaji, just a minute please!' she uttered in a trance-like voice and quickly went inside. She took out the tied handkerchief out of her trunk and came back to the sitting room. She stretched her hand towards Lalaji.

'Lalaji, you entrusted me with this.'

For a minute Lala Hariprasad looked at her intently. She had the rolled up handkerchief with money and her hand was stretched towards him. He slowly took the money from her and bending down kept it at her feet. He then knelt down, took her right hand in his, raised it to his eyes and started sobbing silently, uncontrollably. Her hand was drenched with his tears.

This was a very unusual and peculiar situation, unwanted too. Izzat-un Nisa tried her best to save herself from drowning in the fast flowing river of emotions as she felt the presence of an unseen bizarre sea flowing inside her with the frustrating symptoms of an impending storm. In those dreadful moments, that boy, whom she had met only once after she had got married and whose voice seemed as though it was coming from the depths of the ocean rang in her ears.

'How are you? My eyes have been deprived of your sight.'

Lala stood bewildered for a few minutes and then quickly left.

That night a compelling juxtaposition of colours enveloped Izzat-un Nisa.

Blue, yellow, red, purple, pink, turquoise, ivory, beige, black, pistachio, mauve, grey, lime, rose and blue, all hues of life bathed by the blithe fragrance merging into infinite space and the weather submerged into the wintry fog. Then birds encircled her fragile persona: parrots, sparrows, bulbuls, koels, peacocks, swans, pelicans, falcons. All night she drowned and rose in that turbulent and violent sea. All night the waves tossed her into crests and troughs as if she was a tiny boat. She could feel the presence of somebody flinging her from a forlorn desert to a gushing river; back and forth.

When she woke up, she could clearly recall the colour black, some birds, the turbulent waves of the ocean and the scorching afternoon of a desert.

Something else too happened that day. When she sat in front of the mirror after a bath, she noticed her own reflection and was startled at her appearance, her perfection. Neither the travails of time nor the drudgery of life had impacted her beauty. Long tresses, pinkish complexion, sharp refined features. The smile that adorned her face was self-conscious and apprehensive.

'Bibi, please wear these earrings, they suit you so well.'

Suddenly that distant cousin took over the mirror.

'I am going crazy,' she laughed uninhibitedly.

'Do you have any idea how the entire universe forgets to breathe, when you carelessly push those tresses off your face and laugh?'

'*Ho chukein Ghalib balaayein sab tamaam*
Ek marg e naagah aani aur hai...'
All misfortunes have passed, Ghalib
Just one deathly disaster is yet to come...

... As this long forgotten couplet crawled into her mind and her consciousness reached the second line, the mirror started to form a glittering image of Lala Harihar Prasad.

'Allah, save me from these depraved thoughts.' She moved away from the mirror. But strangely enough she took out a hundred rupee note from the trunk, put on her veil and left for the market.

Another weird thing was her constant deviant thoughts that constantly flew towards Lala Hari Prasad, more so when she was busy cleaning Jalal-uddin. She would be seized by an image ... the image of a man sitting on his haunches, holding her hand and crying. A handsome, dashing man! A gentleman!

She would try her best to dismiss those thoughts by focusing on other tasks but they refused to let go, keeping up a constant game of hide-and-seek with her.

This time, Lala visited after a gap of twenty days.

He did not knock. He entered the haveli at sunset and quietly stood behind the doors. Izzat-un Nisa was busy preparing dinner inside the kitchen. She did not hear any sound, but a sixth sense alerted her and she felt a queer emotion taking over her senses. She left her work and came out. Everything was as usual. Jalal-uddin was lying on his bed, the children were doing their homework in the dim light of the lantern, and her youngest son had fallen asleep. She was relieved and went back to her work.

But within a few minutes, she again felt uneasy.

She was unable to figure out the cause of her heightened nerves. Something drew her eyes to the door. She took a couple of steps towards it. It wasn't fully dark yet ... She recognised him as she reached the door. Lala! Standing quietly!

'Oh, since how long have you been standing? Why didn't you knock?'

'I couldn't gather the courage,' Harihar replied in a desultory tone.

'You are one of a kind, Lalaji. Please come in.'

He followed her into the men's sitting room in the outer part of the haveli and sat down.

'I will be back in five minutes. I have the vegetables simmering on the stove.'

She walked fast towards the kitchen even as she said that.

She quickly placed the tea kettle on the stove, arranged some snacks, she had bought from the market earlier that day in a plate and placed the tea mugs on the tray.

She moved towards the sitting room with the tray of tea and snacks in her hand.

'Oh! Why have you taken the trouble?' Seeing the tray in her hands, Lala said and stood up with folded hands.

'Lalajii!' she said with a laugh.

Izzat-un Nisa's laughter was tinged with sadness.

'This was the least of my troubles.'

She said with a bit of stress on 'least'.

'Bibi, you can punish me whichever way you want, but it was never my intention to hurt you.'

Izzat-un Nisa laughed aloud after ages. For a moment it felt like the dark clouds of her tribulations had cleared up. This was the first time that Harihar stayed for long, almost an hour and a half. This was the first time, the conversation swayed towards her own folks, her maternal home. And it swayed in a way that she completely lost track of how she travelled from the desolate desert of her present surroundings to the soft and cool shade of her past. The conversation took her back to her maternal home where she ran recklessly into long-forgotten rooms, verandahs and courtyards. She saw a monkey dance with fierce abandon in the alley. The thoughts of her loving mother, her adoring sisters, friends, relatives, neighbours, her doting brothers, took her into the realm of euphoria. The time and place she encountered was calm, entering her very being with a peaceful tranquillity like the light and cool drizzle of an early monsoon on parched earth....

Izzat-un Nisa poured her heart out and Lala listened, his eyes not once moving away from her face.

The muezzin's call from a nearby mosque for *isha* prayers jolted her out of her reverie, 'Oh, so much time has passed?'

Lala stood up with folded hands, 'I am so sorry for taking up so much of your time.'

'No, Harihar, you have released me from the clutches of time after decades,' she thought but did not say anything.

Lala stood up and slowly walked towards the door. Izzat-un Nisa was waiting to bolt the door finally for the night after he left. As Lala stepped on the threshold, he stopped, stepped back a little and came closer to Izzat-un Nisa. She noted his proximity with incredible wonder.

'Can I say something?' Lala's voice was tense, laboured.

'Say it please.' she said with the wonder and anticipation still in her voice.

'You will not mind, I hope?'

'Did I mind anything you said until now?'

'Promise me, that you won't stop me from coming to your house.'

'Who else comes, by the way?"

'Should I say it?'

'Please do.'

'I want to see you, to my heart's content, in the brilliance of the sun!'

'But how is it possible?'

'Why? What's so wrong with it?'

'You must try to understand. It is true that no relatives from my parents' side or my in-laws are left to enquire about my welfare or to even hold me for any digression as they have all migrated to Pakistan. But, the houses in the neighbourhood have been handed over to refugees. It is also a fact that all our old acquaintances, familiar with Jalal-uddin's rage and atrocious behaviour, have distanced themselves with a certain enmity in their hearts and now that we are in this sorry state, it is quite obvious that they will be waiting for a chance for revenge. In spite of this, there are some poor houses left in the alleys. Their daughters come to study in my house. Sometimes their sisters and mothers also visit in the daytime as they are scared of the refugees. Then how can I ask you to come in the daytime?'

Suddenly Lala went down on his knees. He was facing Izzat-un Nisa and both his hands were stuck together, 'Bibi! I will die. I need some breath, some fresh air.'

In the symphony of his tone, there was a powerful and unmistakable blend of tears..

Izzat-un Nisa felt that the man on his knees was not Lala Hariprasad. He was a thirsty bird longing for a sip of water in the scorching afternoon sun. She felt like ... For the first time she felt like ...

She bent over Hariprasad's forehead in a trance as though she was intoxicated. Both her hands were eager to cup his face. She felt herself bending, shivering with anxiety.

In that kneeling posture, Lala's eyes were focused on her face in a manner which suggested the yearning in the eyes of a farmer upon sighting a cloud after long months of extreme drought.

Bibi's face leaned towards Lala and his craving eyes.

This sight was witnessed by the glittering darkness, viewed by the encircling haveli, felt by that corner of the sky whose imperceptible tent had stretched over them.

But the spectacle changed within a moment.

Bibi suddenly stopped even as she was bending towards Lala's forehead. With tremendous effort, she slowly stood up and pleaded piteously.

'Lala, please don't make it more difficult for me; I already have enough on my plate as it is.'

Lala stood up with urgent anxiety. Izzat-un Nisa's tears were glistening on his hands, sparkling like gems. He lifted his hands towards his parched lips and kissed her tears. His voice reached her, traversing an infinity, 'Bibi, may your enemies be doomed to death. Why should you burden yourself with so much responsibility?'

'Please leave now, I can't bear it anymore,' Izzat-un Nisa pleaded with folded hands.

Lala looked ever more distressed. 'It's okay Bibi. I am leaving.'

He took a few steps, stopped and then turned. He slowly uttered, 'Please take this.' Hariprasad extended a packet towards her.

'What's this?'

'I am confident you will not reject my devotion.' There was a tinge of softness in his tone.

She quietly smiled, 'Okay. Khuda Hafiz!'

Bolting the door, she came to a room where neither her children nor her husband were present. She opened the packet. There was a saree along with clothes for the children and an envelope with five hundred rupees. All of a sudden she remembered that a month had passed since Lala gave her the money last time.

'Oh God! what should I do,' she muttered to herself.

Izzat-un Nisa never found an answer to this question.

However Lala came back after a week. She opened the door to let him in, but unexpectedly Lala kept standing at the threshold.

'Why are you standing here? Why aren't you coming in?'

'No, I will not come inside. Please read this letter.'

Lala extended an envelope towards her, turned around and with quick long strides merged into the darkness of the night.

Izzat-un Nisa brightened the flame of the lantern upon entering the room.

'I feel like a culprit, I have no right to take advantage of your vulnerable position. I want to serve you and that I will do till I am alive. Your happiness alone will be the reward of this service. I just need some breath and a little fresh air.'

Lala Harihar Prasad
Peeli Kothi
Bypass road
Last house on the second street from the first left turn.
Available hours: 11 am to 2 pm. Wednesday and Sunday.
The next day was Sunday.

Bibi Izzat-un Nisa returned home around three in the afternoon. She was wearing the saree which Lala had gifted her.

When she entered her house, she saw a neighbourhood woman waiting for her. Same day there was *milaad shareef* at her place after the evening prayers.

She took out an old saree bought by Jalal-uddin to wear for the *milaad shareef*. She got ready and reached there slightly before time.

The moist eyes of the listeners were a proof of her passionate and intense recital. Her own eyes welled up with tears which were unstoppable.

She was crying and singing with an exhilarated communion...
Please save me from the wrath of God on the day of judgment....
I am most miserable and unfortunate, O, prophet of Allah..!

—*Translated by Huma Mirza*

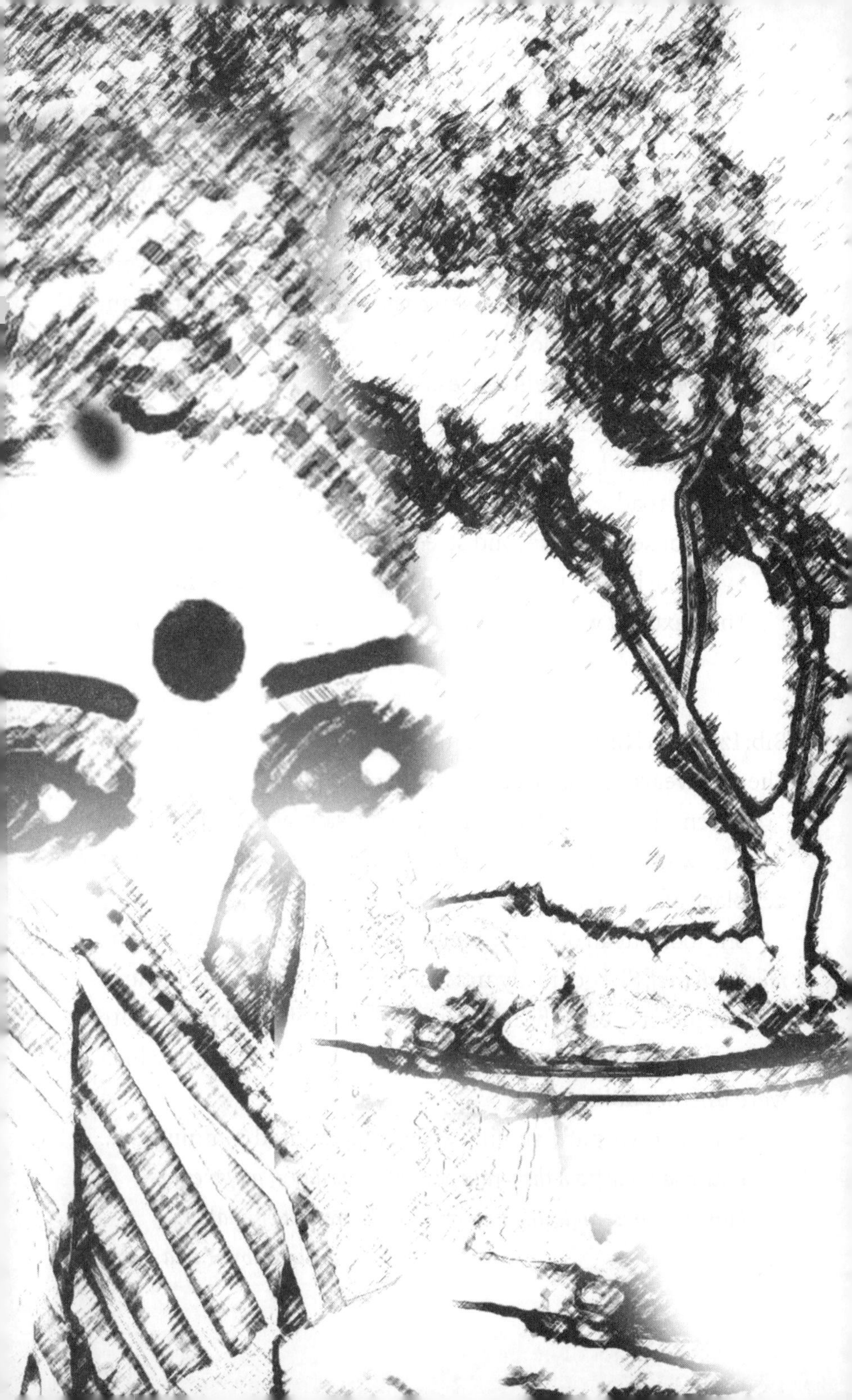

A Bit Odd

Zamiruddin Ahmad

'**Where** has she gone?'

'In the room. Where else would she go? There is only this verandah, or else the room.'

'I mean, what has she gone to do?'

'To change her clothes.'

'Why?'

'First she will take off her puja clothes, only then ...'

'Where have you landed me?'

'Why? What's wrong?'

'What sort of a joke is this? Her mother-in-law is here in the courtyard ... it *is* her mother-in-law, isn't it?'

'Yes.'

'... is sitting here and her daughter as well, and in front of them we will be going inside!'

'So what?'

'Nothing, but it does feel a bit odd.'

'What is there to feel odd about? You are saying it as though this is something new for these people.'

'It may not be new for them, but it is for me.'

'Maybe for you, but not for me.'

'Have you come here before?'

'Not once, but several times.'

'What if her husband shows up?'

'He won't.'

'Wasn't the girl saying, "Papa has gone to the market; he will be back shortly."'

'She said whatever she was told to say.'

'Who told her to say that?'

'Her mother; who else?'

'Did she not want us to come?'

'It might have been something like that; or else, she may have been putting on airs.'

'Why would she put on airs? After all, she called us.'

'Why wouldn't she call us; it is a matter of fifty rupees.'

'Fifty rupees?'

'What else? This isn't G. B. Road. And did you not see the booty.'

'She looked like good stuff, but fifty rupees?'

'And, then, there are two of us: twenty-five for you and twenty-five for me.'

'I don't have twenty-five rupees.'

'Don't worry; how much do you have?'

'May be ten or fifteen at the most.'

'I will pay the rest.'

'There won't be any swindling here, will there?'

'What kind of swindle?'

'I mean, maybe she is a whore and has rented a house and set up her own establishment.'

'What about the mother-in-law and daughter, then?'

'She may be her madam or her mother; after all, don't whores have mothers? And the girl could be her own daughter or even a younger sister.'

'Does this old hag look like a madam to you? Look here, I have told you this is a totally private business; I even know her husband.'
'How?'
'I have known him from Sialkot.'
'Really?'
'The two of us were together in school.'
'No wonder!'
'No wonder what?'
'That's why she told the girl to tell you her father isn't there.'
'No, she doesn't know that I know her husband. Brijinder had brought me here one day and the next time I came here, I met her husband.'
'And you still come here?'
'Yes. Why not?'
'Doesn't her husband — who is your friend — feel bad?'
'What is there to feel bad? She is a saleable commodity. In any case, he is no longer my friend; we were friends in school.'
'Has she been in the trade for a long time?'
'I doubt it; she is still an amateur. That is why I like her.'
'I too think she is shy.'
'I like her shyness. Whores don't have this quality. She is first-class stuff. You will find out for yourself; see the way she shies away.'
'This shyness is hardly a good business strategy. I am finding everything here dripping with artificiality.'
'Such as?'
'All this puja-*paath*. When you first asked the girl where her mother was and she said she was performing puja, my first reaction was to turn around and go away. My second reaction was to laugh out loud ... She whose search has brought us from so far

away is busy performing puja! Surely, we have travelled at least ten or twelve miles to come here.'

'Do you know where we are?'

'I don't know a thing! You've made me drink so much!'

'We are in Shahdara ... it is across the Jamuna.'

'And when we entered the house, we found that whatever the girl had said was true.'

'What did the girl say?'

'Where is your brain?'

'Why is she taking so long to change her clothes?'

'What am I saying?'

'What?'

'What did we see when we entered the house?'

'What?'

'When we entered the house, we saw that the lady of the house was indeed busy in her puja-*paath*.'

'So?'

'And with such concentration that she took no notice of her clients.'

'Yes.'

'What is this if not artifice?'

'It isn't artifice; she does her puja with full concentration.'

'Yes, and then proceeds to sleep with some man.'

'So what?'

'It seems a bit odd, that's all.'

'You've drunk too much.'

'You are a fool. So what if I have drunk too much ... First she serves God and then people like us. It just seems a bit odd.'

'You are talking such nonsense! What good comes from serving God? She will get fifty rupees after serving us.'

A Bit Odd: Zamiruddin Ahmad

'But she might look upon these fifty rupees as the fruit of her labour in pleasing her god.'

'It is her wish; she can see it as she pleases.'

'I will say it again: All this is one big show! All this puja-*paath*!'

'All right, all right! Think what you want ... Come on, get up now ... Let us go.'

'Where?'

'Inside the room. Where else?'

'But she hasn't come out as yet.'

'See, look there ... she has opened one panel of her door. It is signal to tell us that the line is clear.'

'Is that so? But what if her husband shows up?'

'Why are you killing yourself worrying about him? I told you he won't come. He always goes away to the market on such occasions.'

'Shall we enter the room together?'

'Yes.'

'That feels a bit odd.'

'You are finding everything odd! Will you come, or not?'

'All right, let's go. But isn't the god's idol also in her room?'

'So what? It's the only room they have. And you need the best possible room for god.'

'But what if god were taken out and kept in the courtyard for that time, wouldn't that be...?'

'Will you come, or not? It is her house, it is her god. What right do we have to go about placing Him here or there?'

'All right, let's go then. We will place a cloth over god's idol, or else it will feel a bit odd.'

—*Translated by Rakhshanda Jalil*

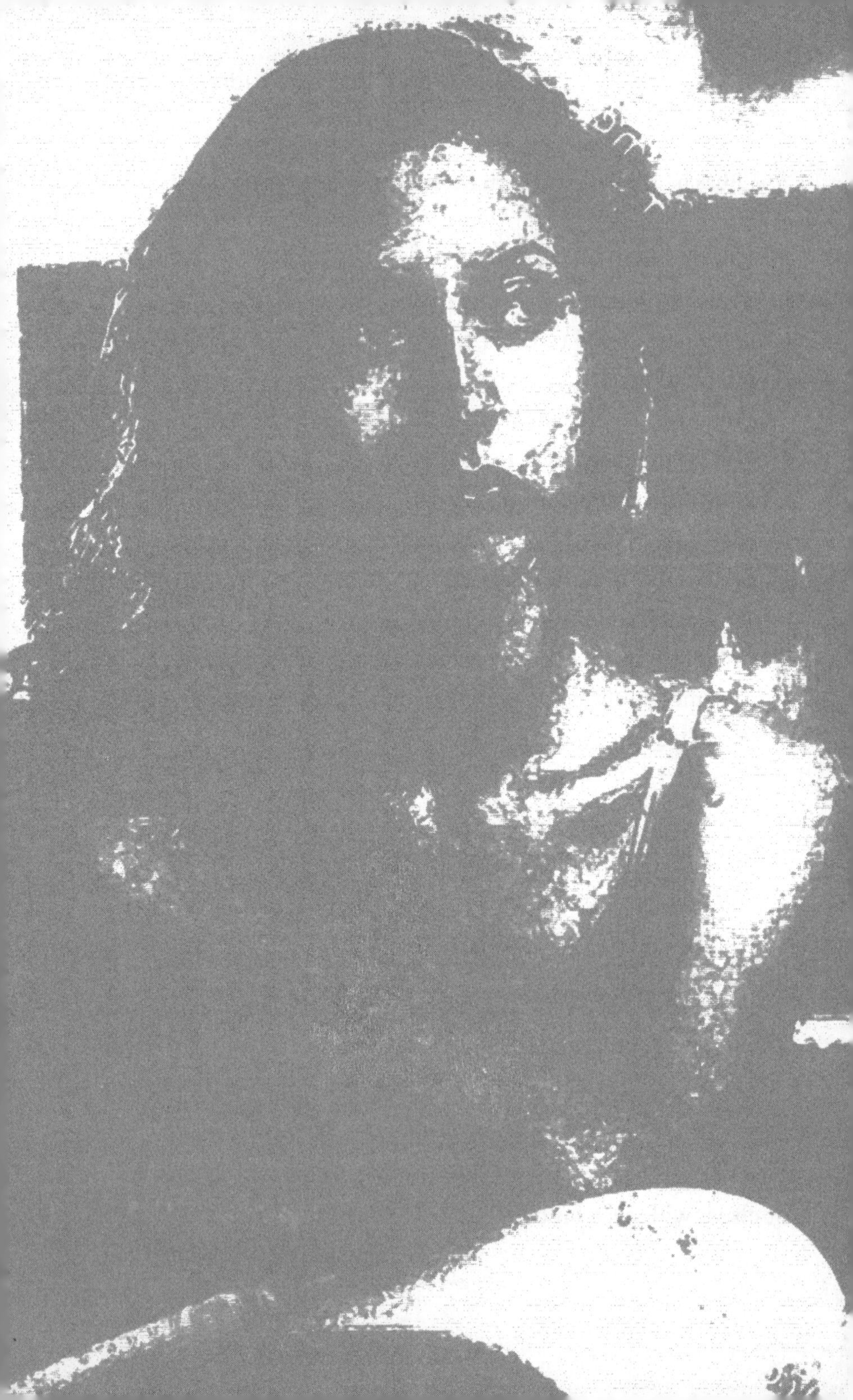

Ash in the Fire

Abdus Samad

More *than ever* before, *I realise* that I am not the same person I once was.

What can I say if I am asked to speak the truth about my existence? That is exactly the problem vexing me at present. I cannot honestly say that I am the same person I was before. I had no choice but to suffer a radical transformation of identity. My compulsions have changed me significantly. I have assumed another identity. It has entered my being, replacing the earlier one. But since it is alien to the identity I was born with, I feel a nagging pain and am wracked with a hopeless confusion as to who I really am. The transformation happened so suddenly and swiftly that I couldn't control or comprehend it.

Who am I, then?

Shall I speak the truth?

Or tell a lie?

No one except me knows the severity of the identity crisis that has been wracking me of late. Should I reveal to others my real self or the one that has been trying to subsume the real one and replace it?

Inevitable as it is, it is not easy to tell people that they must not take me as they think. Painting henna on the palm of a woman, and applying *sindoor* in her *maang*, are not bare customs to announce that she is married. An important chapter of the history of mankind lies hidden behind these acts, and I haven't yet leafed through the book. I have lost the sense that makes one feel the existence of one's own self, or that of others. The strings that jingle to tune with a touch are entirely absent from the innermost depth of my being. What my employers are thinking of me is blatantly unfair, not to me, but to him whom they have entrusted under the care of a tormented soul like me.

I have lost the colour of life!

My strings have lost their tunes, and have become lifeless!

I am the one who lives, but is not in any way capable of giving life to others!

Can anyone with such a state of existence be said to be alive?

And they have hired me to serve a man who has been in a persistent vegetative state for a long time.

In fact, they consider a walking skeleton of flesh and bones like me a living being. They do not believe me, even when I tell them repeatedly that they are completely mistaken about me. I know it more than them, what it means to be really alive. And therefore, I can say quite confidently that ...

The night is wrapped in darkness, but the room is so well lit that some errant rays have escaped out of the window breaking up the darkness outside. At times, I suspect that the night hasn't yet arrived. But the burning in my eyes, and the formidable stillness stretching off into the distance, belie my suspicion. I am performing my duty. My job is very demanding. Had my financial condition been better, I would not have accepted it. I the only reason I am doing this is because it is paying me beyond all expectations.

The pale-faced man lying still on the bed before me is not only young and fairly handsome, but is also seemingly quite healthy. He is a very wealthy man, with a large family. He has everything in the world — a young wife, beautiful children, well-to-do brothers and sisters, rich relatives, and loyal servants. He must surely have been the cynosure of all eyes when he was conscious and active with his brow glowing with youth.

I am sure he always had people at his beck and call, his one sneeze making them worry about his health, his happiness making them all happy, and his sorrow making them grieve. But now, it seems those realities have been consigned to the pages of history, forgotten and soiled.

Though he is alive, he is worse than the dead. He has to be fed to be kept alive. He cannot stir nor speak. He has no sensation, no feeling and no movement. He can only breathe, which is the solitary proof that he is not dead. He is lying on his bed, staring at everything blankly, unblinkingly. He is no more in charge of his life. That charge has been handed over to me though there were attendants who would have attended to all his needs. In the beginning, he was in the care of the members of his family until he became a burden for them. They started looking for a young girl, a creature made of flesh and blood, one who works like a well-oiled machine but has no feelings, no sensations, no flicker of emotion in her eyes. They wanted a cold fish. They wanted her to internalise his feelings and his needs, to live her life for his existence, to sacrifice her pleasures and pains, her entire existence for his survival. Obviously, this meant they had to spend a lot, to make anyone accept a job like that.

I still have my youth, my intelligence, my ambition to conquer the world, my courage and conviction to face all sorts of danger.

But I only lacked in one thing. I was so wretchedly penniless and distraught that I was living an insignificant and unwelcome existence. To overcome that shortcoming, I agreed to surrender my freedom to the servitude of a comatose man.

On my first night of duty, when the night had almost run its course, I inspected my invalid charge who was lying motionless in his bed. The man looked dead, like an Egyptian mummy. I was not used to lying awake late into the night, but the responsibilities of my job didn't allow me the pleasure I enjoyed in my earlier life. I had bargained away my habits, my thoughts and feelings, my fancies, and my time. I had to honour that commitment. So I fed him on time, gave him medicine, and put him to sleep, closing his eyelids. His wife had asked me to call her in the next room if the need arose. I felt increasingly inclined to sleep and go to my bed, which was placed in one corner of the room.

There were only two souls breathing in the room in the gloomy atmosphere of the silent, still night.

A young girl and a very handsome young man!

One physically charged!

The other physically unexcitable!

A discomforting thought flashed through my mind for a fraction of a second, and then darted off. I had lost the right to even think about myself. I had willingly forfeited that right, in return for a generous payment every month. The young man was my patient now, and my only duty was to look after him, with all my body and soul.

It suddenly seemed to me as if he was feeling uneasy. But no, it was my illusion. There was no movement in him. Perhaps he had

Ash in the Fire: Abdus Samad

wet himself, and needed a change, immediately. The doctor had warned that if he was left wet for too long, he would be exposed to severe infection. I got up unintentionally, but stood rooted to the spot. A strange shiver ran through my spine. Did I have to change the man's clothes? So what if he could not move; he had a man's body nevertheless? I had never imagined I would have to do this when I had locked my thoughts and feelings with money. But I had accepted the responsibility to serve him. Why then should I feel ashamed in changing his clothes?

My steps kept moving back and forth. I decided something at one moment, and then drew back the next. Something inside me tried to stop me from making the move. There was no time for hesitation. I must do something fast to clean him. I was a nurse. I should not allow myself to be swayed by my feelings. I was going to get a huge payment for my services so I must forget everything else, and start doing that which could keep my patient alive and healthy.

The man had to be unclothed. His body had to be wiped clean with a damp cloth, and then dressed in new clothes. No one else could do it other than his own wife. What if they blamed me unfairly for handling him wrongly when she or his other relatives saw me cleaning him? I instantly decided to call his wife.

She had locked her door from inside. After many knocks and bangs the door opened; the woman stared at me with bleary, sleep-filled eyes.

'Madam, Saheb needs a change of clothes,' I told her, trying to control my nervousness.

'So ...?' There was a trace of bitterness in her tone.

Her behaviour embarrassed me but I kept my cool and explained to her, 'His body has to be cleaned and re-clothed.'

141

'What do we pay *you* for? You're a highly paid nurse!'

I could not understand what she meant to say. Of course, I was paid a very high salary. Did that mean that I had to do all that a wife alone is expected to do? Did I have to bare the man naked before me? Didn't she know that I was a young, unmarried girl, and still she was asking me to unclothe her husband? What if he was in coma, the hope of his recovery had not yet died!

'Listen, I am feeling very tired and sleepy! Please go and do the job yourself. And tell me if you want more money for that.'

The woman concluded, closing the conversation and the door. There was now nothing left to think about. The patient had been lying wet in bed for quite some time. With every passing moment, he was becoming increasingly susceptible to infection.

Responding to the call of duty, I took on the unpleasant, but essential task, with complete care and concern. I started undressing him. Unfastening the string of his pyjama, my fingers trembled constantly. I hadn't even undone the pyjama strings of my younger brothers in their childhood.

Awe and embarrassment seized me when my eyes fell on his naked lower half. I hadn't ever imagined that the bare body of a young man could be like that. A veil of mist obscured my sight for a moment. Just about that time, a strong stench emanating from his body brought me to my senses. I covered my nose and prepared to go ahead with the task at hand.

Forgetting everything else, I devoted my full attention to cleaning his body, from top to bottom, rubbing it with a wet towel and a little soap, rinsing the lather from it, drying it clean with a dry towel, and finally dressing it in fresh clothes. I also rubbed scented oil into his hair. During the entire operation, he kept staring at me, with his eyes wide open. His pupils were sound and sharp. It was his eyes which always proclaimed that he was alive.

I was deluded into thinking that he was looking at me. This flight of fancy spread a tingling sensation in my body. He, after all, was a young man, with a very attractive physique. If he recovered from his affliction, the whole household would be ready to sacrifice their entire wealth for his one look. He would certainly then try to save his look from falling on anybody as ordinary as me. But sadly, his body lay abandoned with an unknown disease, and his looks had lost their value.

Suddenly, I was transformed into a different personality. It was very different from the young unmarried girl that I was. This changed person in me had now become quite oblivious of those feelings and sensations that have beset her a few moments ago. I was transformed into a caring woman, full of sympathy for the miserable man, who could neither laugh nor cry, who didn't know when he got dirty and when he was cleaned. What was the difference between him and an infant? Although, I hadn't yet nursed little children, I could still feel like a mother. I cleaned and clothed that toy of a man. A strange motherly feeling rose rapidly in me, and I started rubbing my hand softly against his forehead.

The next morning, his wife came to the room but I tried to look away.

Giving me a grateful look, she said, 'You did us a great favour last night. You have actually lifted a great burden from our shoulders.'

'I've only done my duty, madam. There's nothing to be grateful about,' I responded in a low voice.

'Of course it is a favour! We have paid others too to attend to him, but nobody did that job.'

I kept silent because I did not have any answer for her.

She continued her talk in a soft voice, 'I didn't help you deliberately, last night. I wanted to see what you were going to do by yourself. And you have succeeded in your test. I am now relieved that the patient is in safe hands.'

I did not respond; just looked at her blankly. Perhaps my silence gave her some unsolicited message.

'Don't worry about money! We have no objection if you ask for an increase in the salary. I am sure you will take the best care of this patient,' she went ahead with conviction in her voice.

The woman's overly friendly disposition towards me didn't surprise me. I fully understood what she meant to say. Her message to me was that I should now take full charge of the patient, and no one was going to assist me in the job. Till now my job was to only help them in nursing the patient. But now his care had become only my responsibility. They might choose not to help me at all. I had now sold my services fully and willingly.

I am taking care of him as one tends a child — washing him, cleaning him, feeding him, and changing his clothes. I do not take him as a toy because toys do not have lively pupils. He is not yet dead because he still breathes.

I sometimes ask myself that if he had sensations, could I have dared to touch his fingers so easily. The man has everything that can attract a young woman. His attraction to me is albeit more powerful. It is irresistible and obvious. The man has no secrets now. I have laid it all bare. I hadn't ever seen the naked body of a young man, so close to me. I know only too well how feelings and desires came flooding into my mind and how I pushed them back. I have to take on the challenge, and demonstrate that my personal emotions do not come in way of my performance of the services I have committed myself to. I try to fight the young, infirm, emotional girl within me, asserting to myself that I am a strong, responsible, duty-conscious person, and I must overcome my weaknesses. The constant struggle between my two selves and the realisation of my ultimate failure has weakened my resolve.

His family members have now almost stopped visiting him. Once in a while, they just peep in to ask about his wellbeing. I, nevertheless, give his daily health report to his wife, without being asked to do so. I feel quite satisfied in doing that. It gives me strength to feel that I am discharging my duties properly and faithfully. This comforting thought fills me with the ecstasy of triumph and renews my vigour. I set out on my mission with the fresh hope of suppressing the weak, emotionally afflicted girl living inside me.

But wanton thoughts have wings that can help them fly, unrestrained. I fail to clip their wings, in spite of my repeated efforts. These thoughts perch on my mind, and fly out, leaving a mysterious flavour that relishes my entire being. I try to chase them away. They do disappear, but only momentarily, and again come back, giving me a tingling sensation. My body is soaked in tiny beads of sweat, and I am incapable of thinking rationally. A solid wall of sensations stands erect before me, and obscures my vision.

When the man lies exposed before me, in the state in which not even a transparent veil of silk can hide him from my eyes, a vagrant thought crosses my mind. What if at this very moment, his consciousness, his sensations return to him for a while, just for a while ...?

I had passed, every moment of my time, through a very hard test. But up till now, things had appeared according to my expectations. I didn't, however, know what the future held for me. I had thought that my everyday duties would repeat themselves without any sudden change, and being used to them, I would go on succeeding in my effort to put a check on my feelings. What I didn't know was that there were more difficult situations ahead, waiting for me.

One night the insensitive toy left under my care, fell down from his bed. Not even a faint sound escaped his mouth. I was sleeping dead in my bed after a very long and tiring day. When I got up the next morning, I saw him lying on the floor like a dead body. My heart sank, and perhaps missed a beat. I felt his pulse. Thanks God, it was beating. It was not possible for me to lift him, and put him back in his bed. I ran out fast and called his wife and other relatives. They reacted in a very odd way when they saw him lying like that on the floor. Their eyes bore deep into mine, as if I was solely to be blamed for the accident. I could not decide how to answer their hard stares. My only mistake was that I couldn't immediately attend to him when he fell. Had I not been tired from working long hours, I wouldn't have slept so deeply. Anyway, I put him back in his bed with their help, and requested his wife to be there beside her husband and sleep there for the night to avert another accident.

'Don't we give you a lot of money for the job? Why this negligence, then? He fell from the bed and you were sleeping carelessly!' the woman complained bitterly, ignoring my suggestion.

I had no answers for her. But then, I thought I shouldn't take it silently, and spoke out slowly after a few moments, 'I am always nursing and caring for him, madam. Had I been awake, this would never have happened.'

'Surely you have to look after him even when you are asleep?' pat came her curt reply.

'How can I do both, madam?' I asked.

'Simple! Why don't you sleep in his bed beside him? Drag his bed along the wall. Let him lie on the side of the wall, and you sleep on the other side. He'll be safe, then.'

Perhaps she had premeditated this suggestion. I gazed at her in astonishment.

What was the woman saying? She was asking me, a stranger, to sleep with her husband. Granted, the man was lying senseless and still, but he was still alive with a healthy body, available to be used as he preferred. No one had a right to it without his assent. On the other hand, the man's nurse was a living person, a stranger to him, and not senseless like him. Didn't she realise that she was going to play a dangerous game?

I was not a bonded slave. I could have refused to work there, and escape whenever I wished. I had sold my services, and not my self-esteem. But I knew for sure, that if I really left my job, the man would be totally neglected, and left to die. They were, anyway, waiting impatiently for his death. They had taken everything that they wanted from him. He had nothing left now to be given to them. His life was useless for them. Their appointment of a caretaker for him was just a formality, which they were compelled to dispense with. They had to show to the world that they were looking after him well. I believed they might have killed him, hadn't I taken up the job of nursing him. I had sacrificed my heart and mind, my comfort and pleasure to serve him, and he was no more than just a patient to me. I had tried to give him a new life — a life of care, warmth, and delicate touches. And as long as he breathed, the hope of his recovery remained alive.

It was not possible for me to abandon him.

They were very happy when I agreed to their bizarre suggestion. The bed was quickly adjusted according to the plan, and the patient was moved to the side of the wall. Looking clearly pleased, the woman set my pillow and all on the other side of the bed, quite willingly allowing me to sleep beside her spent husband. She had consigned him to my charge, completely, thoughtlessly, believing as though she had bought a machine, which didn't have any emotions and feelings, and which could do any job, mechanically with the push of a button. Perhaps my silence too convinced them that I was no more than just a robot. None of them realised that I too had a heart that beat, a mind that thought, senses that could respond, sensations that could affect my body, and a body that was virgin and sensitive.

I spent the first night restlessly, sleeping with him in his bed.

I am at a loss to explain how I spent it. It passed in a state of deep anxiety and a great inner turmoil.

I have now become used to sleeping with him, after the first ordeal that gave me the lesson of my life and transformed my whole being.

Ash in the Fire: Abdus Samad

In the lives of unmarried girls, there comes a night, their first, when they no more remain single. It is this night whose dream they start chasing, designing and decorating since the time, when all the colours of the rainbows start adorning their eyelashes. Colours must have decorated my dreams too, but I had never imagined my dreams would find such an interpretation.

My ward is the possessor of a well-built and attractive body. Its sheer magnetism can send currents running through other's bodies. I try to muster enough courage and composure, and get on with my job clearing my mind of every stray thought. I address all his needs throughout the day, put him to sleep at night, close the door, switch off the lights, and then induce myself to sleep beside him. Something, though, tries to stop me from doing the last job, every night. Every night, I slump in the armchair near the bed, till late, holding a book, and leafing through its pages. My eyes refuse to stay on the printed words, and a hazy mist swirls in front of me.

A strong feeling overpowers me every night — the feeling that I have to sleep with a stranger. It's true he is senseless, but I am not. Those who compelled me to do that cared only about his needs; they cared less about my feelings. It's also true that the enormous weight of a huge salary has pressed down my feelings. But what will happen if a fierce and fretful storm sweeps that heavy weight away?

I needn't blame others. Why should I look up to them to consider my sentiments, my feelings? I know it only too well that my anxieties are not going to help me out of the situation. The fact of the case is that I alone am responsible for accepting their offer. They would never have hanged me for refusing to accept it. I, therefore, must put the objective, my duty and not my ego, before my eyes.

The night goes on with its journey, and though my eyes burn with sleep, my eyelids stand in revolt. A pale shade of green light hangs in the room. He lies in an unconscious state in his bed, with me by his side. His face, his entire body in fact, is clearly visible even in the faint light. He has a personality, which can undoubtedly draw people's attention over and over again. Had he not gone into a coma, they would have looked at him not with pity, but with respect and desire.

I try my best to keep a respectful distance from the man, while sleeping beside him. But though I can afford to be careful because I was conscious and waking, he may not. His senses are out of his control; his limbs do not move at will.

His hands and legs touch mine repeatedly in sleep. A strange but not disagreeable sensation runs down my spine every night. In a remote, forgotten corner of my heart, an unfamiliar desire erupts out, and fills my being. It induces me to let his limbs touch my body, even if it is for a short while only. But this entire urge evaporates as it comes.

The call of duty supersedes that of desire, and I remove his hands and feet from over my body, very carefully. The thought that I am all alone, and there is nobody there to help me out of the awkward situation, suddenly comes to my mind. I consider myself as a flower ripped apart, fallen from its branch and fated to be trampled down.

It was on such a night when I was sleeping fitfully with my heart throbbing with fear, even in my dream, that he might come closer again and put his limbs over me, or I might out of ecstasy get closer to him, and ...

Between those fits of sleep and waking, when I came to my senses, and probed into the secrets of my mind, the truth dawned upon me that it was not the throb of fear, but of longing. I felt I was waiting for the touch.

It was the first chapter of the story that ended with a momentous change in my personality. I had to realise with awe and acceptance that from now onwards I had to go through the same experience every night.

I looked at him with an unintentional smile when I got up the next morning. Surprisingly, I could only catch the glimpse of a vague smile feebly playing on his lips. I could not give meaning to it, though one could easily discover some sense behind mine.

I had tried to hide many facts behind my smile. It had helped me in displaying a calm and composed face which could steer me through many difficult days ahead. My smile was a kind of impregnable fortification against the rising tide of feelings from inside.

My fretful nights started their journey from then on.

Whether I am waking or sleeping, the strange flame of desire keeps burning in my eyes, and I restlessly wait for its fulfilment. I watch him sleeping like a corpse every night, and start counting down to the time when he would stretch his limbs and they come into contact with my body. And when it really happens a war starts inside me between my call of duty and the assault of deepening intoxication. At long last the call of duty defeats inebriation, and tolls me back to my rational self.

Sometimes the wait becomes long and distressing, with no end in sight.

The intoxication wrought upon me by my desires and sensations, overwhelms my being, and I become silent and still, until I realise that this silence is a sin. I must act, wriggle out of it, and free myself.

Sometimes, I think what will happen to me if the man recovers and gains back his consciousness.

He is the first man in my life with whom I have been spending my nights. No curtain comes between us. I have seen all. I have nurtured his body, washed, and cleaned it. I don't know if anybody can serve him better than me even after receiving twice as much as given to me.

It is strange how a relationship which has no meaning and no sanction creates its own place in the mind, secretly, silently, and strengthens its roots there.

I wonder how the vacuum, created after the tingling sensations peter out, will be filled. Can I completely free my mind from them? Can I scrub them out from my inside?

Then, one day it so happened that on becoming extremely tired after nursing him and cleaning the room, I tumbled into the bed and drifted into deep sleep. I don't remember what part of night it was; I felt an extraordinary, mystifying pleasure, even in that dream-like state. Suddenly, I woke up with a jerk, and found the delightful sensation still possessing me in my conscious state. I was so intoxicated with those sensations that I couldn't realise for some time as to what had caused it. I recovered my consciousness fully well, after a good while, only to realise that the light and welcome drizzle of pleasing sensations was coming from the touch of his heavy hand, which lay stretched on my tender breasts.

A strong current ran through my body.

My immediate normal reaction at that time would have been to push away his hand, control myself, and get out of the bed even for a short while. But I did nothing like that. And in spite of being struck by the strong current, I didn't writhe or quiver. I kept lying there, surrendering myself to the sensations that it had produced in me. The apprehension that his lost senses might come to life after this electric touch, crossed my mind. Though I knew it well that his hand had fallen on my body quite unintentionally, I was apprehensive of its staying there for so long. Who knew and who would check if it started moving and doing other jobs, inadvertently though?

Was I waiting for him to proceed and do more?

I held my breath, waiting for the next move.

Nothing happened … nothing happened for quite long, except that my mind whirled and a mysterious, though delicate, feeling of being unsafe surrounded me from all around.

Was I an object with whom anyone could do whatever one wished? I should have pushed him aside and got away.

Instead of doing that, I reminded myself again and again that he had not done the act knowingly. Had it been so, it would not have stopped and stayed at one place, and in one direction, and for so long. I suspended all my thoughts and feelings, and stayed there without a stir, watching what was going to happen the next moment.

I had my body fully clothed. Besides my undergarments, I had worn a *salwar suit* made of thick cloth, and had covered the upper part of my body with a *dupatta*. Perhaps that was the reason

153

why the heat from his hand didn't reach my body, but only a firm pressure maintained itself, taking me on an excursion to strange worlds. I was restlessly waiting for his other hand and the rest of his body parts to move without any intention, and touch me all through my being. How I wished nothing would have changed, and I had stayed longer lying like that!

It was after a long, long state of stillness that I realised that his hand kept on pressing me with the same pressure — never increasing or decreasing. To call it a pressure is rather misleading. It was just heavy, a male heaviness.

I tried to lift his hand slowly. It dangled in my hands, like a soft but heavy snake reaching to bite me. Terrified, I left it and it fell lifeless by his side. I quickly touched his forehead with my palm.

There was nothing there, no warmth, no pulsation, only coldness, a deathly coldness that seeped into my bones, through his body.

I admit I am no longer what I used to be till some time ago. I have become so stiff and senseless that even if countless needles are pricked into my body I would not stir or shriek with pain. Run strong electric currents through my body and you will never see the slightest movement or sensation in it! The tingling sensations, those delicate feelings that I had always considered my existence, and preserved passionately as my identity, have gone away with the wind, leaving me with the naked frosty reality of existence.

The feeling that I was taking delight from the touch of a dead man's body has killed my former passionate self forever. All my desires, feelings and longings, have burnt with the experience of that one restless, eventful night. Anything of the past, any feeling or curious sensation left hiding behind the four walls of my heart, about which I am not aware, is ready to be consigned to the funeral pyre.

I don't know if I am still alive. If you call the existence of passionate, warm, pulsating desires, an irresistible longing for the touch of a hand, and a warm hug, as the sole proof of life, then I am worse than the dead. I have turned cold and senseless.

I am in a state of flux.

I am no more of any use for the living.

A strong sense of sin erodes my mind.

Should I stay in my job or run away, quietly?

The war raging inside my being, and my belief that I had won it, was all a delusion. In fact, I have lost all wars, on all fronts.

How can I live now?

Why should I live at all?

They want to offer a throne to a defeated girl.

How should I make them understand they are making a gross mistake?

—*Translated by Syed Sarwar Hussain*

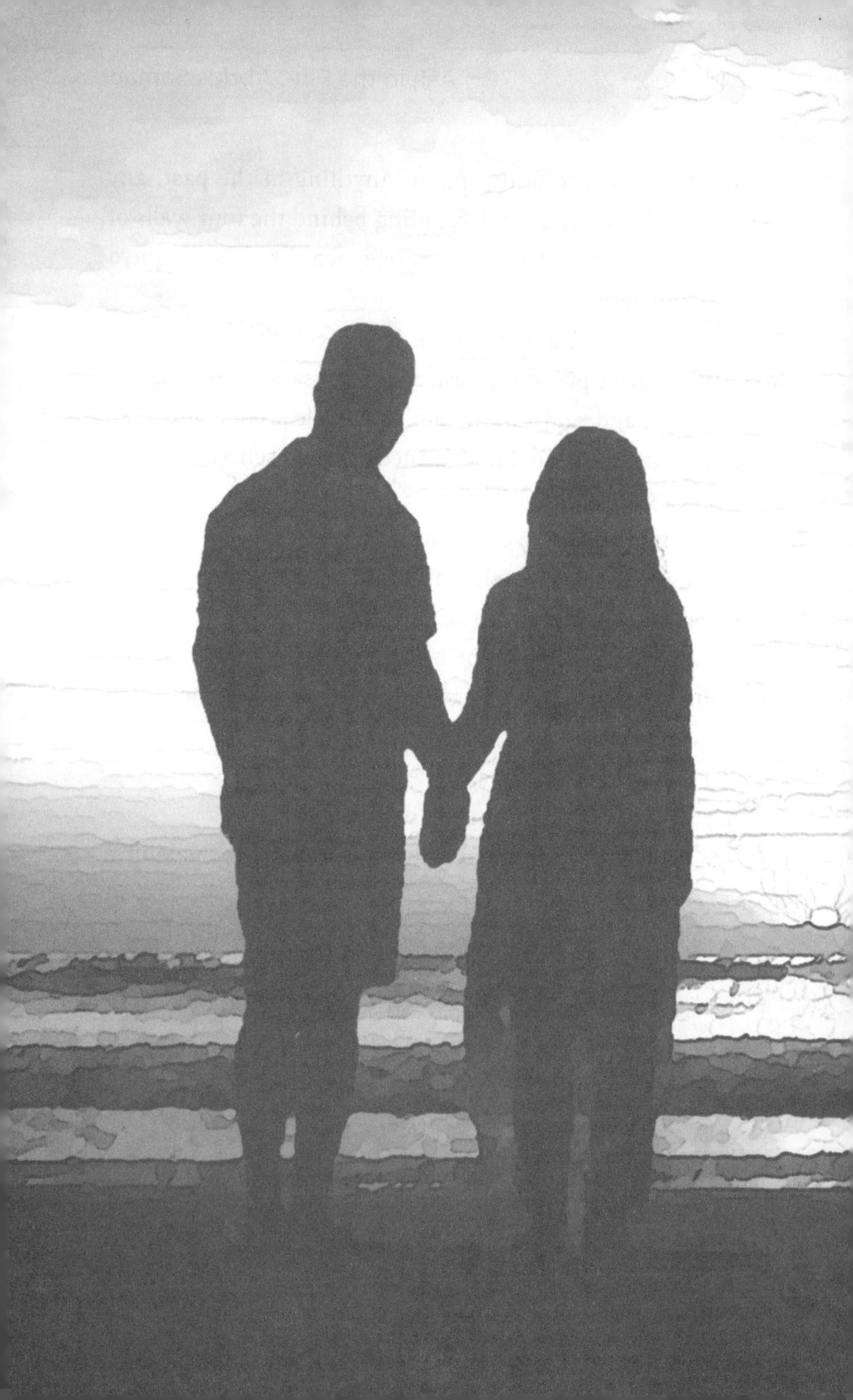

Asexual

Rahman Abbas

It was the month of May. The sun was unleashing its heat on Mumbai. A vapour was rising from the belly of the earth and it seemed that the tar of the roads would simply melt away. Shahid Iqbal wondered if this city was sitting on the sizzling fuse of a firecracker whose heat from inside the surface was turning the roads hot. Wiping his face with a handkerchief he entered the college's registration office.

Placing the documents inside a file, the clerk told him that the college would reopen from June 10.

Shahid Iqbal reached the college late on the morning of June 10. The Principal was addressing the students. Everyone had introduced themselves already. Standing at the threshold of the classroom, when he looked at the Principal, he felt as though his shoes were stuck to the hot coal tar of the roads. She gestured that he enter the classroom. The Parsi Principal continued speaking about the methods of teaching.

Within two months Shahid Iqbal became friendly with most students at his college. He was nominated for the college cultural committee. Teachers also started liking him. Everything happened the way things happen and stating those incidents is not the intention of this story. Whatever has been narrated so far is only to establish a backdrop. The real story starts from here.

There was a girl in his class. She used to sit at such an angle that Shahid Iqbal could not see her face clearly. She never spoke to Shahid and neither did she participate in any of the activities where Shahid might participate or where she might have to speak to him. Shahid found this somewhat strange. Shahid even mentioned this to his girlfriend and said, 'Why is she so wary of me?'

'It's simply your idle imagination. It's possible she takes no interest in you,' his girlfriend told him.

'But barring me she mixes around with everyone, smiles, speaks to them,' Shahid countered.

'That's her wish. Don't assume that she thinks of you as her adversary,' his girlfriend tried reasoning with him. When she found the topic boring, she said: 'Forget it.'

👁 👁

Even while sleeping with his girlfriend in a hotel, the strings of his consciousness remained attuned to the thought of Tasneem Deshmukh, the girl who always ignored him. She always sat at an angle from where her face wouldn't be visible to Shahid. She would never go where he would be present. He was not sure why Tasneem kept hovering over his mind for long. Gradually, Tasneem became an intolerable vortex on the screen of his mind. He started wondering whether Tasneem disliked him, whether she hated him. He wondered why his heart did not have the strength to tolerate the fact that someone might bear hatred towards him. He became angry. He wondered why rejection from someone annoyed him so much. He would pick up Tasneem and throw her in the Arabian Sea, if he could. Bury her under the earth.

Asexual: Rahman Abbas

This situation became intolerable for Shahid. He was bewildered. Every time these thoughts traversed his mind at the speed of light, he would be in a miserable state of discontent, confusion and existential crisis. So heightened was his mental conflict and turbulence that he could not even enjoy sex to the full with his girlfriend.

In the fourth month, the college picnic was finalised. Shahid was in charge of it. He was convinced that this time he had a perfectly valid reason to approach Tasneem. In the course of collecting fees for the picnic when he called out Tasneem's roll number, a reply came from far, 'No!'

This utterance came like a storm and caught him in its grasp. His face turned ashen. A loathing for Tasneem took root inside him. However, he kept his calm and remained silent. Stunned, he kept looking at her. She was busy reading something.

That evening he spent three hours with his girlfriend in a rented room but he couldn't free his mind from the disagreement with his own self.

About ten minutes to go before they left for the picnic trip, a sudden surprise awaited Shahid. Tasneem was standing in front of him. She had a bag in her hand.

'Janab, I'm coming along for the very reasons I gave earlier declining to come,' she said.

Barely able to say anything to her, unable to even understand, he was perplexed. He said nothing. Just as he was about to utter something, she was already inside the bus.

Making merry, singing loudly, screaming and shouting, the students were now headed towards a hill station about four hours away from the city. Among a few that were sitting solemn and quiet, Shahid was one, although this behaviour was contrary to his nature. Tasneem was sitting in the very last row with her friends. Shahid's own silence recreated a very old scene in his head from many years ago where, he was at the seaside with his first girlfriend Hina, in torrential rain, getting drenched sitting on the sand. The heaving sea had converted into shimmering mercury. In the low light, this moment had evoked a sense of permanence for them. They had wished for this inexpressible feeling to become eternal. In the throes of passion when he had kept his lips on Hina's breast, the fragrance of her body had spread inside the labyrinth of his being.

Today, despite all detachment, hidden desires were spilling out of the same dark labyrinth of his heart and reflecting a new form in his eyes. By this time the bus had reached its destination. It stopped in front of two bungalows.

The girls went inside one bungalow, and the boys inside the other. After some refreshments, Shahid lay down. But he wasn't sleepy. He felt like reading something. Taking out a collection of stories by Roald Dahl from his bag he started reading the well known story where the boy speaks to animals. But even this magical story couldn't engage him. The topic that he was interested in was in his mind, but clearly there was no way it could voice itself. Just then the Principal instructed everyone to get ready to go see a waterfall.

The bus stopped at a spot near the base of the waterfall. Camera clicks started freezing the waterfall into different moments. The entire spot was covered with mist. Tasneem was gazing at the ravine standing atop a large rock. Drenched in mist, the thick cluster of trees in the ravine looked enchanting. Shahid went up to Tasneem. Approaching her he said: 'Can I talk to you?' Tasneem stared back at him blankly. She didn't say anything.

'What are you watching?'

'Forest and darkness.'

'But it isn't dark yet.'

She stood silent.

'By the way, how did you like the waterfall?' Shahid tried to steer the conversation forward.

'Beautiful but bereft of purpose.'

'How's that possible?'

'The water that we see falling, it doesn't stay in the same place the very moment we see it.' Shahid would have said something in response but a teacher's voice came trailing. The train of conversation was broken. At the teacher's voice, Tasneem turned away and Shahid kept watching the waterfall for a few moments.

Everyone were to cook dinner together. The boys were chopping meat, the girls were chopping vegetables. They indulged in pranks and mischief while at work. Amid all this Shahid was thinking had he continued to speak to Tasneem, what all could he ask her. On the other side, while chopping vegetables with her friends, Tasneem too was lost deep in thoughts.

After dinner, the Principal summoned everyone for an evening of fun and games. Boys imitated the girls, jokes were told, and girls on their part mimicked the boys and also other forms of mimicry.

The programme ended after midnight. Everyone proceeded to rest. Tasneem had vanished earlier. Shahid couldn't see her. He went to his room and sat on a chair in the balcony. Loud conversation and laughter streamed in from the bungalow where the girls were staying. There was another commotion within Shahid which was not subsiding. He told himself that Tasneem did not hate him. Maybe she was a pessimist. A strange person. Wish their conversation had continued longer, he thought. Thus the night lengthened, caught in this desire of knowing and not knowing. However, this time, instead of disintegration and chaos, the thoughts in his mind flowed on in a pleasant wave. This was a kind of music whereby he could even sense the presence of insects in the dark around him.

The next morning, around ten, everyone went for a stroll outdoors.

The girls rushed excitedly at the sight of flowers and butterflies around them, and the boys enjoyed looking at them. Tasneem was walking at a slow pace. Shahid was walking alongside a teacher, speaking to him. Seeing Tasneem trailing behind everybody, his own speed reduced. He caught up with her and they walked together.

'Pleasant weather, isn't it?' Shahid said.

'The weather here is usually nice.'

Shahid was at loss as to how to take this conversation further.

'I always wanted to talk to you, but ...'

'But what?'

'I felt that you deliberately ignored me.'

'Yes, I did.'

They walked in silence.

Preparations started around three in the afternoon for their return trip.

On reaching the city, the Principal allowed the students to alight from the bus wherever they wished. After a while as the bus traversed some distance, Tasneem too got down with two of her friends. Shahid turned and saw her receding fast with the trees and other people in the background. He wondered even if she was a strange girl, she could at least talk to him. Only when I talk to her will I know what she is, and how she is, was all what he could ponder.

The next day was a holiday. Shahid spent this day with his girlfriend in a hotel room, but this time he had little interest in intercourse. There was an inexplicable reflection in his mind and he searched for its meaning. So much so that he even forgot that he had to be present that evening at a function organised to discuss the implementations of reprieves suggested by a commission probing the Mumbai riots. He had forgotten several things. If at all he remembered anything, it was that particular strain of conversation he had with Tasneem, where it had got snapped.

Tasneem didn't attend college for two consecutive days. Shahid was upset, disturbed. But on the early morning of the third day, seeing Tasneem seated in the first row, he felt a sense of relief.

He sat behind her.

He was sure that Tasneem will turn back and see him. Then he will exchange courtesies with her. She will thank him. He will then ask her to have tea with him. She will turn down the offer. Then he will press her to come along. Finally she will give in. During tea he will discuss literature with her, present her with the book of her favourite novelist. Then they will meet by the sea. He kept on imagining thus, but that day, no such interaction took place.

She didn't go to the canteen to drink tea, rather kept sitting glued to her desk. College hours ended. Other than just watch her, Shahid did nothing else. She collected books from the library and started for home. Shahid stood with his friends looking at her. He called out her name in a loud voice. As he went up to her she told him not to call out so loudly.

'Why? What's the matter?'

'I'm deaf to loudness .... I don't hear loud voices,' she said in a low tone.

She left while Shahid remained standing like a statue. And truly now he himself couldn't hear any of the commotion around him. The debates, cross-talk of friends, the din of cars plying on the road — nothing reached his ears as though something within him had been switched off.

He no longer tried meeting Tasneem.

But he'd sit at a spot from where he could observe her. Her neck, back, the hair falling around her shoulders.

After a week or so when he was sitting in the class reading a book, Tasneem went past him enquiring how he was and that she'd like to speak to him during recess. Immediately he began feeling happy and began revelling in the earlier imagination that had lost all charge. There were two more lectures to go before recess started, but time seemed to crawl. He wondered what Tasneem would ask him, what reply would he give, if she'd agree to befriend him, etc. All his thoughts took a backseat when right after sitting down with him at the canteen, Tasneem asked, 'Are you ill?'

'No, I'm fine. Absolutely fine. Why do you think so?'

'I haven't seen a book in your hands these past few days.'

Shahid took this as an opportunity to frame a reply.

'I'm trying to read you these days.'

'What!' Tasneem exclaimed.

'My statement is not a vague one,' Shahid said, and watching Tasneem's reaction, he added, 'I'm trying to understand you.'

'I'm not a symbolic story. In fact, I'm not a symbol of myself.'

'Listen, I don't get what you're saying, but I like listening to you. I simply want to understand this ambiguity.'

'In this life it's a miracle if we can understand ourselves. So, it's okay if you don't understand me. I don't wish you to.'

'But it's possible I may wish to,' Shahid said.

She remained silent.

Shahid drank his tea.

'You talk in riddles,' Shahid said, breaking the silence.

'Ambiguity is also rediscovery.'

'How could we inquire about ourselves in the obscure haze of our vague ideas?'

'The imagination that we have about our own selves is also a kind of ambiguity. That's why every individual stresses upon their own interpretation of being true. While others reject them.'

'I always feel that you've been rejecting me. Is it true?'

'No. Rather it is true that I identify myself through you.'

'What do you mean?'

'I was impressed with you.'

This sentence made Shahid very happy, the way a child becomes happy when a top is lassoed and thrown in and it spins at a great speed.

'But I'm devoid of any feeling of attachment,' Tasneem said.

The spinning top suddenly toppled over.

'You were impressed by me and yet you can't have any inclination towards me. This, this is rather hard to believe.'

'No, it's true, and even if I want to, it won't be possible for me.'

Saying this she stood up, went up to the counter, paid the bill, and walked out of the canteen.

Shahid kept sitting right there, losing the ability to hear any of the commotion around him. There were a lot of puzzles in his heart and there was no chain of words in his mind whereby he could capture a single idea. Why are ideas in opposition to words? He too left the canteen.

Tasneem was waiting for him outside. He went towards her. His eyes were on her footsteps and his heart was not in his control. They walked up to Byculla railway station. All along they were silent. As the train arrived, Tasneem glanced at Shahid once and got into the train. Shahid kept standing. Several trains left.

The college was closed for three days. Bal Thackeray was supposed to have been arrested. He wasn't.

When the college reopened Shahid was in the teacher's common room preparing a seminar report. Tasneem came into the room and immediately saw him. She went up to a teacher. At that very moment the teacher called out to Shahid. He turned and both his and Tasneem's eyes met. He felt a certain warmth in his own eyes.

'Hand over that list to her,' the teacher told Shahid.

The teacher's sentence acted as a pebble thrown in a still lake. The ripples extended in both their eyes and stopped at their heart's beat.

'Alright, sir,' Shahid said.

Handing over the list to Tasneem he said, 'I missed you a lot in the last few days.'

She said nothing.

'I wanted to speak to you,' Shahid continued.

There was a faint smile on Tasneem's face.

'Even I felt something akin to that,' Tasneem said in a suppressed voice.

'Oh, I can't believe this,' Shahid said in a spurt of effusion.

'Felt the same with a few other boys,' Tasneem said, interrupting Shahid's sentence.

The expression of thrill on Shahid's face changed to sadness.

Composing himself he said, 'Yes it happens.'

'I want to see the sea,' Tasneem said.

'I'm attracted to the sea, rain, snow and rivers.' Tasneem paused for a moment, looked at Shahid and then continued. 'Something happens to me whenever I'm near the sea. The waves pull me in. I can't control myself.'

Shahid listened to her in surprise.

'Land has a strange relationship with water, isn't it?' Tasneem took off her spectacles and watch and placed them in her bag. She took off her shoes and then started walking towards the sea.

Shahid kept watching her. She went into knee-deep water and turned around. There was happiness on her face. She waded in further. This time the waves were around her waist. Shahid couldn't keep waiting in the shore any longer. He ran up to her in the water and said, 'You never know, these waves.'

Tasneem wanted to go further in but he stood blocking her way. At that moment a high wave came and Tasneem staggered in its force. Shahid caught hold of her hand and started pulling her back. Both of them fell into the water. Back on their feet again they shivered from being wet all through.

'It feels so good, doesn't it?' Tasneem said.

They kept running in the water, catching hold of each other, and falling down, and floating and dipping in the waves. They emerged from the sea after an hour. The sun was shining bright on the sand particles. They sat on one side of the shore.

'*Yaar*, I'm sorry, my hand ...' Shahid said.

'What?'

'My hands touched your breast once by mistake.'

'I didn't feel a thing,' Tasneem replied immediately.

She paused. Then she thought for a moment and said, 'I don't feel anything.'

Shahid kept looking at her.

After a brief silence she said, 'You must be thinking what sort of a girl I am that kept frolicking in the sea with you all this while.'

'It made me happy. I never thought you would,' Shahid said.

'When did I think I would?' Tasneem stood up and began walking. Shahid followed her.

The sand wasn't too hot and the sea lay sprawled in a siesta.

They went to the sea several times together after this. Now they spoke more to each other.

Shahid also kept meeting his girlfriend during this period and they even slept together several times.

It was the beginning of autumn. The gulmohar tress were naked. Dry leaves remained scattered all around. In the afternoons the leaves would gather and rush in the breeze from this side to that. It produced a strange soft melody. With the warmth of such a dulcet music in his heart, Shahid went to Mumbai University campus to meet Tasneem. After having tea in the canteen they came out and sat at a desk. They discussed politics, education, literature, and their friends. After a brief silent phase Shahid said, 'Don't you think I like you a lot?'

'I know it.'

'So much so ... that I even want to marry ...'

'I know that too. I know you want to marry me.'

'And you?'

'Even if I do, there isn't much I can do.'

'Why?'

She stared blankly at the leafless trees.

'Why, is it your family ...' Shahid asked.

'No, it's not that.'

'Then what is it?'

'Listen, when in the class I sat at a place from where you won't be seen, when I declined to come to the picnic, when we were watching the waterfall, on the night of the picnic when you had performed in the programme, the next day when we were walking together, then when you had turned around to see me as I got down from the bus, when we spoke at the college canteen — from then onward I've been feeling a connection with you. A kind of an inexplicable tie,' she said it all in a single breath.

They kept sitting at the desk and in the background the falling leaves made their own music.

Tasneem spoke again. 'Despite my longing, despite my love for you, what could I do even if I wanted.'

Shahid held both her hands and said, 'What's the matter?'

She kept silent.

Tasneem then looked at the ground scattered with the greying-brown leaves and said, 'I don't feel any need. I'm a dry river.'

Shahid cupped her hands in his own. But there was no response in those hands.

Shahid kissed her hands. He saw her eyes had welled up with tears.

The noise of the fallen leaves in the backdrop took over the scene.

They were at the same spot. Seen from the great height of the sky, it is possible that they appeared like two little dots.

—Translation from the Devnagri version of the original Urdu story by Nabina Das

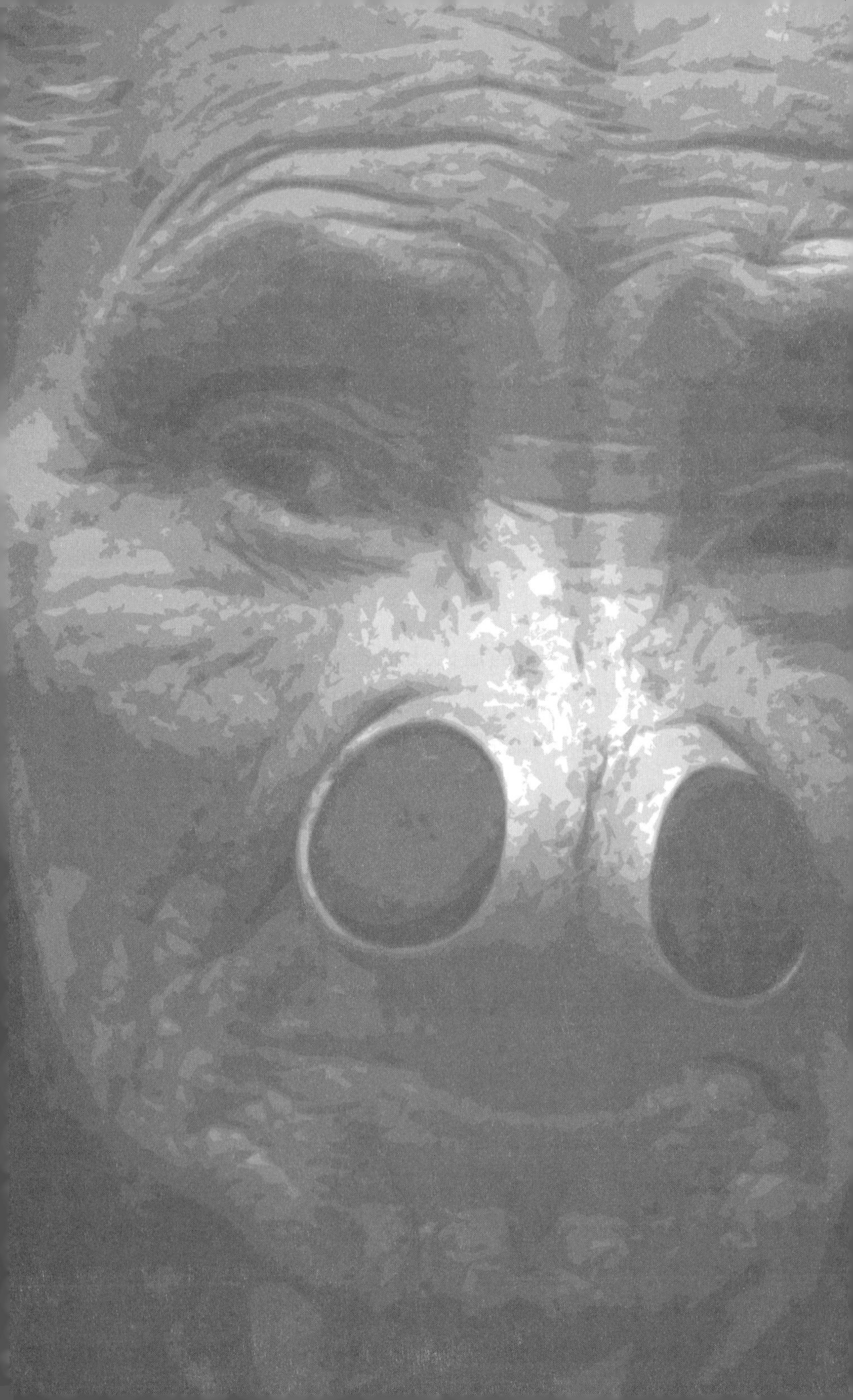

The Well of Serpents

Siddique Alam

Sitting all by herself under a teakwood tree, the girl was making lines on the forest floor. She held a shrivelled twig between her fingers. Every once in a while the twig would snap but she would restart her work with what remained of the stump. The work was not being done absentmindedly. Soon the lines took on the shape of a big cauldron full of water. Though there was no fire burning under the cauldron smoke was emanating from the watery surface. The girl must have realised this lacuna for she started drawing some faggots under the vessel. This was not a difficult task but once the pile of faggots was formed she kept staring at it for a long time. How long? It might be ten or thirty minutes, or a year, or perhaps a century. She came out of her daydream and without setting fire to the faggots threw away her twig. She rested the back of her head against the tree trunk.

The breeze was browsing through the tree tops. Given her posture her ample bosom protruded upward and her long black hair cascaded down her back as if a headless body lay under the tree.

Time passed by slowly. The horn of a motorcycle broke the silence. The revving of the engine continued for a while before it stopped. After a brief silence the sound of leaves being trampled upon was heard. Yet her eyes remained closed. A few minutes later she felt a peremptory tap on her right shoulder and opened her eyes. A tall lanky boy stood bending upon her. He had removed his dark glasses.

'This is not a safe place. You must not come here alone.'

'I am not alone.' She raised herself but instead of looking at him hugged her knees with her arms and peered into the interior of the forest where tree-trunks stood shimmering in the rays of the sun pouring in through the gaps in the leafy branches. 'I am never alone here.'

👁 👁

This was the era of steam engines, when ashes and smoke ruled the world.

My uncle was an employee of the Indian Railways and after every three or four years he would be transferred to some remote station. In those days he had been driving his train to the iron ore mines of Odisha hidden somewhere among the mountains. Since we had no other place to go we would visit him as soon we got a chance.

In those days he had been posted in a place where the most attractive thing for me was a giant well whose walls were made of iron. Its water was meant to be pumped into steam engines. When I peered inside all I could see at the bottom of the well was the dark water that was reflecting a part of the sky. At first glance, one could see only the crescent of the sky rolling inside but on observing keenly one could see a number of snakes slithering there. An iron ladder spiralling along the wall went straight into the water, its rungs jutting out. Most of them were broken and hung from the wall precariously. In high summer when everything on the earth looked wilted and moribund the well would give off a foul smell that might be of the excreta of the hawks and ravens that perched for hours on end on the rungs of the ladder or maybe it was the stench of the polluted water itself where snakes slithered. I was scared to think what would happen if someone fell headlong, right among the snakes. It was too horrible to imagine.

'Nothing like that has ever happened.' My uncle chuckled at my morbid imagination. We used to call him Rail Abba as he was an engine driver. 'But of course a story can be fabricated. Perhaps you firmly believe in such stories the way I see you staring into the well for hours on end.'

Rail Abba had a curly beard growing over his full cheeks which he had dyed red. His teeth were as colourless as old copper as if over the years his dentures had also been coated with dust and ash. Or maybe it was because of his addiction to smoking; he was a chain smoker. He had on a cotton cap, a gift from an Anglo-Indian guard. It had been blackened by the smoke from the engine. Thanks to that Anglo-Indian guard, Rail Abba was an inveterate drunkard too.

Though Rail Abba was a heavily built man there was something else about him that intrigued me. On his right arm the name of his paramour was tattooed in Hindi. A mysterious female eye ringed this name which had been written in Devnagri script. The eye was adorned with long attractive lashes. Though all through her conjugal life she had been seeing this eye. my aunt showed no interest in it as if it were none of her business. Maybe she had no idea of what was written. Or maybe, like other women of that era, she didn't care much about such things. One day Angora, the elder daughter of Rail Abba, whispered in my ear that the name belonged to a tribal woman. She had learnt that language during her school days in Rail Abba's last place of posting as it was the only medium of learning there. Later, on his transfer to a new place, not only had her knowledge of the language withered away, her education itself came to a permanent halt.

'I know this woman,' I lied. 'I think I have seen her. A jet black witch! She used to come to our home to sell things!'

I was hoping that I would win her favour by planting this myth.

'Doesn't she come now?'

'Let me think.' I closed my eyes and tried to recall those rustic women whom in my childhood I might have seen with my uncle. There was no trace of such a woman as far as I could remember. Being tired of this exercise I opened my eyes and said. 'No. She does not."

'Then why would he get this name tattooed on his arm?' Angora asked casting a furtive look at me. It was strange that it was she who was asking me this question whereas she was four years older than me. Didn't she know that once a name is tattooed on a human body it can never be erased? You are bound to live your entire life with it. I was thinking of telling her this fact when suddenly she looked into my eyes. 'You know what happens between a man and woman when they are alone?'

'Whatever it is, take it from me it would not be a good thing.' I replied. It was an age when women used to shy away at the sight of men and it was their fate to be beaten by them every other day. It was a drama we would come across every day in farms and fields.

The Well of Serpents: Siddique Alam

'But if Abba has got a woman's named tattooed on his arm there must be some good enough reason for it.' Angora gripped my forearms tight. 'Maybe someday you too will get someone's name tattooed on your arm.'

'So what's it to you?' I tried to retrieve my arms.

'Because you are a crook! You never look me straight in the eyes.' Her fingers became tighter and her nails started biting into my skin. I had no other recourse but to examine her physique at very close quarters. But that was not possible as she was standing too close. The proximity of her body made me dizzy. Not only had she become prematurely adolescent, but her dresses were unable to rein in her growth..

'What are you doing, are you crazy?" I scratched my head. After all she was my sister and I was not very comfortable being so close to her.

'I want to feel your eyes on me,' she said and after releasing my arms began walking towards the quarters of the railway station. The roofs of the quarters were overgrown with grass and archaic clay chimneys stood atop them like questions marks. Later these chimneys would disappear when new quarters would be made for the railway employees. I looked at those chimneys from which coal smoke was emanating and rubbed my arms which displayed the conspicuous red marks left by her nails. I assured myself: Don't worry. Some day you will get replies to all your questions.

Though that mysterious eye tattooed on the arm of Rail Abba has been haunting me from my childhood, I had no idea whether it was on account of Angora's words or due to the fact that I had come in contact with her young body. No sooner had I returned to our native town than I began to search for that tribal woman who was said to have had an amorous affair with Rail Abba. I looked closely at all the tribal women who moved along the road outside the railway station. A little further down that road our two-storied hut stood mirrored by a pond, a corner of which was fully choked with water chestnuts. Usually the tribal women would be either those coming from the countryside to sell milk or women with baskets full of plastic bangles inlaid with lac. Some of these rustic women would be seen with baskets poised on their head, baskets that were full of live snakes. These women would amble along the dirt road moving towards the leather godowns from where an unbearable stench was carried down by the breeze. Once in a while, a woman would be seen carrying an entire bee hive on her head with honey bees crawling all over it. Then, there was an old woman. What set her apart from the others were her breasts, hanging low on both sides of her navel. She would appear with a basket stuffed with roosters raised for cock fights. One of my distant relatives, the one who had a grocery shop located near an abandoned indigo factory, used to buy roosters from her. He had the temperament of a maulvi who chewed betel leaf all the time and every other day would predict the arrival of doomsday with very convincing signs. But he had a weakness for cock fights from his school days. He would train those cockerels and not only sell them at a good premium but also personally take part in the cock fight that took place in the village fairs. At the outskirts of our town, there was a weekly *haat* where staging of cock fights was a regular phenomenon. In these fights drunken old men would routinely bet all their earnings. My uncle was an integral part in these events.

'Do you know the story of this woman?' One day he asked me, looking pensively at his lopped off ring finger. Four years ago he had lost it during a cock fight. The blade tied to the leg of a fighting cock had slashed through it while he was soothing the bird.

'What story?'

'Her husband was a born drunkard which is a common phenomenon among these forest dwellers.' He removed his skull cap and scratched his head. His hair was grey and reminded one of rotten hay with squirrels and rats racing over it. 'One day he was so pressed for money that he sold his wife for a bottle of liquor.'

'Oh no!' I was hanging on to every word now.

'I knew you won't believe it.' He replaced his cap on his head. With his cap on he looked like a scarecrow stuck on a bamboo pole somewhere in the vegetable fields. 'But it did really take place. And do you know, what happened afterwards? She became as faithful to her new master as if he were her husband. He happened to be a magician, expert in conjuring up dead spirits that roamed the jungles. Many of them were his slaves but a few had become his foes too. It so happened one day that one of them hit him so hard that he turned completely deaf in one ear. In this rumpus he caught hold of a sheep and brought it home. The sheep had a red beard and round horns. He told the tribal woman that the sheep was her ex-husband whom he had overcome in a fight and through the force of his magic turned into a sheep.'

'And she believed him?'

'She had no reason not to. It so happened that she became so servile to the sheep that the magician felt cheated. But he was helpless. Not only was he a good-for-nothing sort of fellow, by now he had also developed a soft corner for the woman. He was afraid, too, that if he got rid of the sheep she might leave him for good. As you know, these tribal women are not like our wives who remain faithful to their husbands till their last breath. Not only are they very laborious and self-reliant they are the ones who see to it that their idle husbands are properly taken care of. No wonder these women are always ready to break their tether. But there might be another reason for the magician to be so helpless.'

'Now come on. What could that be?'

'The villagers had taken a liking to the sheep. He was so virile that within two years the entire village was crawling with lambs.'

I was speechless. As far as the psychology of tribal women was concerned I was a complete novice. As far as sheep and goats were concerned, from my childhood days I had been under the impression that the only purpose of their existence was to be knifed by the butchers. I nodded my head in approval. But my movement was so dubious that it could have been interpreted as a shake too. I was under the illusion that by such means I could hoodwink anybody.

But my trick failed me this time. What with his hawkish eye, my uncle had detected my bluff.

'You are not listening properly, are you? You don't believe me. You know I hate lies.' He stared at me in disbelief.

'Yes, I am listening.'

'You don't believe me. You think I am fabricating stories.'

'Why do you think so?'

'I can read your eyes,' he said. 'You are a buffoon. You never reveal what is going on inside your mind. I should have noticed it earlier.'

And he refused to narrate the rest of the story. That day, for the first time, I realised that nothing is more painful in this world than a story half told. Its wound would never heal. I carry that scar to this day. As a consequence I started taking this tribal woman seriously. Though her face was no different from other tribal women her nose set her apart as it was the most prominent thing on her face. The turned up holes of her nostrils had two copper septum rings pierced through them. Though her sunken eyes carried no mystery about them her nipples, surrounded by a copper coloured halo, lay on both sides of her navel in such a way that they looked like two hooded snakes. A closer look revealed white marks akin to the teeth of a viper. Every time I would cast my eyes on them a deadly snake would crawl on my neck. While I stared at them not for a second did it occur to me that I was committing a deadly sin.

The woman must have discovered how interested I was in her. One day I saw her standing near an electric pole outside our house. She directed a weird look at me and before I could fathom her motive stretched forth her bare arm in my direction.

A sheep was tattooed on it with a beard and round horns.

Thereafter I came across her many times. I was curious about the person who had tattooed the animal on her arm but I was afraid I could never make her understand that.

Time passed on and gradually I forgot her. The next time I boarded the train to visit Rail Abba, not only was I alone, but it looked like I had already been transformed into another human being.

Clutching my suitcase as I entered Rail Abba's quarter, I hesitatingly directed a look at Angora who was sitting with her mother in the next room. She had become a bit plump and was avoiding my gaze. Then our eyes met and it dawned on me that I had become irrelevant to her. In my absence something must have happened that had alienated her from me. I was hurt. I had come here with a lot of expectations. I had acquired elaborate knowledge about some extremely forbidden things that could have thrilled her. But here I was ... at a door that was tightly shut on me. However, her changed attitude was not my only worry; a more hopeless incident was awaiting me.

The iron well where snakes used to crawl and which had started haunting me in my dreams had dried up completely. There was no water inside. There was no movement at the bottom. All the snakes had gone.

'It is not a well but a water tank embedded in the earth.' Rail Abba told me when I returned home. He was drunk as usual and was stuffing things inside a wooden box whose blue colour had lost its shine. At sunset he would be heading for the iron ore mountains. 'The last steam engine that used to ply on the tracks has been recalled. You can see it outside the station where it has been kept for public display. The tank is of no use now. Besides, due to low rainfall the pond which was its only source of water has dried up too.'

'And what about the snakes?'

'You know how deadly the heat is here. As the water receded they must have started eating one another. Those that remained alive were attacked by hawks and mountain crows. A few months back you could have seen a few of them crawling in the well as also

The Well of Serpents: Siddique Alam

the snake eaters hovering above them. No sooner would they spy a moribund snake in the well they would swoop down and come out clutching it in their talons.'

Verily it was like Angora. The only difference was she had been lucky enough to escape my claws.

However, my guess about Angora proved right. I soon discovered that she had developed a sexual liaison with a boy whom she would meet at the outskirts of a Sal forest, a few yards away from the railway track. Tall *kasiroo* grasses with their catkins swayed in the fields outside the forest. The boy would turn up on his motor cycle, a *Bullet* that he must have bought from some military personnel in the cantonment. Both would sit on the verandah of the signal man's quarter that had been abandoned and talk for hours on end. One day they found me hovering around the back of the quarter but ignored me altogether as if I were a thing of no consequence.

'You like that boy?' I asked her the next day when we were alone.

'Are you grown up enough to ask such questions?'

'Yes,' I replied. 'I have leant more of this world than you can imagine. Do you have any idea that your father had another woman?'

'Does it make any difference?' She shrugged her shoulders and smiled. 'Now my mother is the only woman he has in the world.'

'Do you really believe in it? Rail Abba spends more of his time with his engine. Though he is no longer a wrestler still he is very macho. And your mother ... she's grown old.'

'Aren't you ashamed to talk about your own aunt like this? And what is it that you want from me? Should I die a premature death by simply mulling over the other woman?' She was furious.

'Had I been in your place I would have found out about that woman.'

'And what for, pray?'

'What rubbish, Angora! It is natural for a child to be curious about these things.'

'Perhaps you are right. But now that you have quizzed me, let me inform you that I am planning to elope with that boy.'

'Why on earth would you do that? Why don't you take up the matter with Rail Abba? I think he will give his consent to the marriage.'

'He will never do such a thing.' She looked straight into my eyes to assess whether I was trustworthy enough. 'He is wanted for a lot of murder cases. The police is always after him.'

'And still you meet this guy?'

'Yes, I do. Do not forget that I am the daughter of a man who has had the name of his paramour tattooed on his arm.'

We saw her mother with her younger sister. They were returning in a rickshaw from the railway market. She was in a veil.

Angora lifted her head and looked at me.

'Do you miss the well?'

'Of course,' I said. 'And also the steam engine that has now become a thing of the past, a mere public exhibit. Throughout my childhood I had been painting this steam engine in my drawing book. I will always miss it on the tracks.'

'Any other disappointment?'

'Yes, I am also disappointed with you. I can see you eloping with a boy on his motorcycle.'

She smiled, showing all her teeth. 'They are right. You really are a buffoon.'

We went there a number of times afterwards. After our last visit, my father was not on good terms with Rail Abba. During school vacations when I asked permission to visit them he simply ignored my request. Two years elapsed. One day we were informed about Angora being possessed by a jinn. But the information had come too late as by that time, thanks to local wizards, she had fully recovered. Despite the fact that the information had come too late, being close relatives, we had a moral obligation to visit them.

I was seeing her after a gap of two years. She was now a fully developed girl, a bit taller than I remembered. She had developed dark circles around her eyes and was spending most of her time sitting silently on her bed or looking vacantly at the outer verandah whose walls were blackened by the heap of coal lying there. This coal would be dumped at the veranda for free by people who stole them from Rail Abba's train.

'You must get her married as soon as possible,' Abba advised Rail Abba. 'And you must also get rid of that woman. I have already warned you but you have no ear to good counsel. Your daughters are growing up. I have been informed that you have an illegitimate son from that woman. Is it so?'

'By God Almighty, I have not seen her for the last ten years. And the boy is nothing but a rumour spread by some mischief monger.'

Abba was aware of his bluff but he had no intention of interfering in such matters. His philosophy was that no one but the person who had gone astray himself can mend matters..

I was sitting by Angora's side, trying to read her face. Squatting on the floor, her mother was emptying out the cotton from a rotten, old quilt. She looked like a woman who had no presence to speak of.

'How come you were possessed by a jinn?' I asked her in a sniggering tone. 'Tell me the truth.'

'Don't laugh at them.' It was as if I had touched a raw nerve. They roam all around us either in the guise of animals or other living things. Aren't you a Muslim? Change your attitude towards them.'

'Do you really see them?' I was amazed at the fluency of her speech. Was she really possessed? Had she learnt all this from her medium?

Angora kept staring at me.

'What is on your mind?' She looked tired. Then she called out to her mother. 'Ma, please tell him to behave.'

'Son, why don't you take Angora out for a walk?' My aunt asked me without looking at me. She was busy squeezing the bed bugs that were running in a disorderly confusion on the floor as soon as they were released from the layers of cotton. 'She never goes out these days.'

'I am not going anywhere.' Angora said in a sulky voice and fell silent. I waited for her mother to leave the room. After she had gone, I enquired in a hushed tone about the boy she used to meet at the signal man's quarter.

'He has not turned up for the last nine months.' She answered lowering her head. 'People say he has been murdered. But it could be a rumour too. Can you find out the truth/?'

'There is no need to waste time. What else could happen to the likes of him?' I declared arrogantly and walked out of the quarter through its back door. Here the place was choked with garbage among which open concrete sewerages snaked out in all directions, their murky water accumulating at their mouth as if they were the maps of different countries. Jumping over the garbage dumps and the sewerages I came up to a dirt road that gradually sloped to a level crossing. I ambled along the railway tracks heading for the forest where at other times the fields would abound with white *kasiroo* flowers. But it was not their season. The fields were bare. The sky was empty, no birds circling it. The leaves of trees that came in my way had started wearing a red and yellow hue. Battered by the wind the leaves were falling gracefully. Autumn had arrived. I left behind the trees that were completely overcome by autumn and stood on a concrete culvert under which water was flowing. I stared at the railway tracks that had been laid out on stones. A few steps ahead, there was the signal man's quarter. Its door and windows had been pilfered and its roof had developed a big hole through which the sky was visible. I was sure that Angora would follow me here.

And I was right. Within five minutes I saw her. She had stopped a few yards from the quarter. Her feet were hidden deep in the grass.

'Why are you standing there staring at me?' I shouted.

She moved forward and reached the verandah where she removed her right slipper. She was cleaning her bare leg on the concrete step of the verandah. She might have soiled it in some shit or dung.

'Why you have come here?' She asked without looking at me.

'I like this place.' I lied. 'Or maybe I wanted to see this place now that that beloved of yours has gone.'

'You rascal! I know very well what's on your mind. Come with me.' She put on her slipper and pointed towards the forest that loomed at the back of the quarter. She was walking carefully on the field. She didn't look back at me or maybe it was not possible for her to do so as the ridge on which she was walking was too narrow for her to turn around. I didn't follow her. While she walked in that clumsy manner I kept staring at the obscene lines her buttocks were drawing on her shirt. For the first time in my life I was feeling the heat of a young female body impinging so frankly on my nerves.

Circling the bushes that grew haphazardly on the uneven slope I walked between the tree trunks. The gaps gradually grew between them. Here the earth was choked with roots and mounds of rotting leaves. I had not gone very deep in the jungle when I saw Angora standing in the patch of sunlight falling from a gap among the branches. She had her ear stuck to the trunk of a teakwood tree. The tree was not very old and its leaves were sparkling. I stood close to her without her knowing. She didn't notice my presence until I startled her.

'What are you doing?'

Her body jerked and she turned towards me. God, I can never forget those eyes! Those were not her eyes but the eyes of a girl whom I was seeing for the first time in my life.

'Why don't you stick your ear to that tree?' She pointed to a tree. It stood right behind me. On inspecting the tree trunk I found that it was rotten to its roots. I looked back at her. She was again standing with her ear stuck to the tree. My tree was not only old but looked like it was about to topple over any day. Red and white ants crawled on its rough bark. I cleaned a portion of it and cautiously placed my left ear on its cracked surface. I heard nothing but the rustling of breeze as it whipped down the trunk of the tree. From the tree top a faint hint of chirping of birds was perceptible.

'Not like that, idiot!' Angora's voice floated across. 'Press your ear hard on the bark. You really are an imbecile, unable to do such a simple thing.'

I pressed my ear on the trunk so hard that its rough bark stung my skin. But come what may, I was not willing to be dubbed an idiot again. And then something strange happened. I perceived some human voices inside the bark. First they were very low and kept vanishing abruptly. Then they would appear with more force as if emanating from the veins of the trunk. It looked like thousands of women and children were shouting and calling out to each other. I was frightened. I removed my ear from the trunk.

'Did you hear the voices?' Angora stood very close to me.

'What are these, Angora? Whose voices are these?' I asked as she stood very close to me.

'You have not yet heard it all.' And she pressed her ear on the other side of my tree trunk. I followed suit sticking my ear to the bark again. Now the voices were clearly audible. I stood stock still staring at Angora whose eyes were shut tight.

'Are these human voices or is it just my imagination?'

'You decide; after all, you don't believe in spirits.' She said as she opened her eyes.

'No, I know this has nothing to do with spirits.' I pressed my ear on another tree trunk. The same voices were audible there, becoming clearer gradually though their tone had changed. Now it seemed as though hundreds of women and children were wailing together. It looked like they were mourning their dead. And now without any effort on my part the voices were coursing their way into my ears.

'The earth is mourning or lamenting for something.' Angora said. 'Do you have any idea what is this lamentation that arises from the depth of the earth?'

'I don't know.' I was shaking like a leaf. Despite her presence or maybe because of it, the loneliness of the forest had deepened. My hair stood on end. At every step I feared that some human hand would rise from the earth and grab my leg.

'What do you make of them?' She bent over me breathing on my neck. To get rid of her, I was pressing my ears from one tree trunk to another.

'I can't understand. What are these?' At last I could no longer walk. I stopped and stared at Angora. My legs were shaking involuntarily. The weird voices were extremely loud buffeting me from all sides. It was time to leave this place as early as possible, I thought.

'Don't you think there are people underneath the earth that you stand upon, hundreds and thousands of them, women and children, all lamenting and wailing and beating their breasts? This howling and beating of breasts, what do you make of these? What incident could have taken place here?'

It was strange. The wailing and lamenting of women and children seemed real now as if the dead had come out of the depths of the earth and, while invisible, were nevertheless moving about!

'Do you hear these voices?'

'Yes.' I replied. Now I could hear the voices without pressing my ears on the tree trunks. 'It scares me, Angora. How do you come here all by yourself? Let us go away from this place. It is not meant for human beings.'

'Really? And what are you afraid of?' She gave a ghoulish laugh. 'This earth is all we have, where else will we go? This has become our destiny. From the beginning of mankind till date billions of people have turned to dust and gone into the making of this earth. How long will we keep away from them? One day we too will be one of them. These people wailing God knows for what, don't you think, once they too had walked on this earth, like you, like me?'

'What do you mean by these things? Let's go. Leave this place.' As she stood in front of me she appeared more mysterious and fearful to me than the forest itself. The entire view before me had become hazy. The sunlight was falling between the leaves in such a manner that the entire forest appeared to be shimmering in water. Walking among the bushes, pits and roots I tried to find an exit from the forest but at every step my leg would sink into the rotten leaves. I would notice it only after my legs were engulfed by them. I wished she would come to my rescue. But I felt she was not there. I turned back. At first she was not visible. But then I caught sight of her. Standing on one leg she rested her back upon a tree trunk. She had kept her other leg folded on the trunk. She was staring at me unblinkingly.

'Coward!' She shouted. 'What are you, a good for nothing!' And she vanished behind the trees.

I came out of the forest, walking under a sky that looked smeared with ashes. I was not going towards the signal man's quarter nor back to the residential quarters atop which the chimneys look like crooked question marks. I crossed the railway tracks and started climbing up the slope. As I scaled it I realised that the earth was ascending like parapets overgrown with scrubs and bushes. At places one or two trees stood under the blue sky as if contorted by rough winds. Only a handful of leaves were left on the branches precariously rustling and making a noise as if they were drawing their last breath. Clambering up the steep slopes of the ascending earth which was perilously narrow at some places, I caught sight of the iron bridge of the station and stopped. Down below, the railway tracks were gleaming in the sunlight while across the barren fields the forest stood mysterious and silent. I had left Angora behind. From here the forest looked denser. There was no movement among the tree tops. And though I was too far from that place I could hear the call of a raven. I have seen these mountain birds. They never call in a bunch as common crows do.

I strode down the path that had emerged from nowhere and headed towards the iron well.

There was not a soul in sight. The well stood alone. I looked inside. With no water at the bottom it looked darker and deeper. But on casting a closer look I was amazed to find that some water had accumulated at the bottom. Could it be on account of some recent rain? I was trying to be sure whether it was water or something else when I discerned some movement there. Clutching at the brim of the well I lowered my head as far as possible, keenly searching in the dark, and as I grew familiar with the darkness I saw a tiny snake gracefully drawing a thin line in the shallow water. As I stood mesmerised I heard a shrill whistle from the sky and looked up.

A hawk had come down very low spreading its majestic wings and, aiming at the well, it was drawing a wide circle in the sky.

—*Translated by Daem*

Glossary

beta: meaning son but used often irrespective of gender for a child

chaadar: meaning a sheet but can also be used for a large shawl to cover a woman's body when she sets out of her house; used instead of a burqa

chappals: slippers, any open, slip-on, flat-heeled form of footwear

doli: a small, covered palanquin carried by two or more men on poles on their shoulders

fajr: the first of the five daily prayers mandatory for all Muslims

firangi: meaning foreigner but used specifically for the colonial British presence in undivided India

iktara: a single-stringed rustic musical instrument

Jat: a member of an agricultural community in the Punjab and parts of northern India

kos: a measure of distance equal to roughly two English miles

mataji: form of address for mother

milaad: a celebration to mark the birth of the Prophet Muhammad with songs and prose passages in praise of his many sterling qualities and the circumstances around his birth; usually held during the day and month of the prophet's birth but also to mark special occasions such as an impending marriage, house warming, etc.

Glossary

mukh: homes in rural Punjab had a portico-like structure in the outer part of the house which served as a living space; food would be cooked in open fires, children would play and most household activities centred here. The rest of the house, even for the prosperous, would comprise only a handful of rooms that served to store goods and commodities or, where household members would sleep in extreme winter

namaz: the Muslim form of prayer offered five times a day, it is an intrinsic part of the Muslim profession of faith
nikaah: the Muslim marriage ceremony
numberdar: also *'lambardar'*, a title given by the colonial powers to landlords who were assigned the task of revenue collection and also maintain law and order at the village level

puja/puja-paath: a Hindu form of worship comprising prayers, songs or readings from scriptures

savan: the second month of the rainy season roughly corresponding with the period from 15 July to 15 August
shabaan: the eighth month of the lunar calendar
suhaag raat: wedding night

thaali: a metal dish to eat from, usually made of copper or an alloy; often it comes with matching small bowls

wuzoo: the ritual ablution mandatory for all Muslims before they offer *namaz*, the five daily prayers

Notes on Contributors

AUTHORS

RAJINDER SINGH BEDI (1915-1984): With *Dana-o-Dam* (1940), his very first collection, Bedi earned a place for himself in the canon of Urdu short stories. Beginning his professional life as a postal clerk, Bedi moved to Bombay and got involved with the film industry like many of his fellow progressives but his interest led him from writing the dialogue and screenplay of over 27 films to producing and directing memorable films like *Garam Coat*, *Dastak* and *Phagun*. Women occupied a central position in a great deal of Bedi's writings and he has etched some memorable female characters: the eponymous Kalyani and Lajwanti, Indu in *Apne Dukh Mujhe De Do*, Rano in *Ek Chadar Maili Si* and Ma in *Banj*. Details of everyday life, no matter how small, found a place in his stories and became reflections of a larger social reality. Bedi's stories survive the test of time because they hinge on the common and the commonplace that transcends time and circumstance. However, the same Bedi who was hailed by the progressives as a champion of their cause because of his portrayal of lower middle-class working people later distanced himself due to his unwillingness to conform to communism and the soviet brand of socialist realism.

KRISHAN CHANDAR (1914-1977): Despite a master's in English and a degree in Law, he went on to become one of Urdu literature's most prolific

Notes on Contributors

writers with over 80 published volumes. Having written innumerable short humorous pieces, romantic short stories, novels, it was the short story that earned him laurels. Accused of being an incorrigible idealist, even a maudlin sentimentalist on occasion, Krishan Chandar was in some ways a 'flawed' progressive. Stories like *'Kalu Bhangi'*, *'Mahalakshmi ka Pul'*, *'Shikast'*, *'Jab Khet Jage'* display his socialist concerns and his heartfelt empathy for the poor and downtrodden; however unlike the other progressives he was seldom able to free himself from despair and defeat. His most prolific period is said to be during 1955-60 when he published the autobiographical *Ek Gadhe ki Sarguzasht* (The Autobiography of a Donkey) in 1957. He remained an active member of the PWA and was held up as a role model for budding progressives.

GULZAR (b. 1934): Poet, author, film-maker and film lyricist, Gulzar is one of the most prominent names in cinema, popular culture and literature in present-day India. Recipient of the Padma Bhushan and the Sahitya Akademi Award, he has also received the Oscar for the song 'Jai ho!' in the Hollywood film *Slumdog Millionaire* in 2008 and the Dadabhai Phalke Award for his contribution to the Indian film industry in 2014. A well-respected name in poetry circles, he has several non-film short story and poetry collections to his credit. He has recently published his translations of Rabindranath Tagore and has written poetry especially for children.

FAIYAZ RIFFAT (b. 1940): Born in Etawah, UP he has done an MA in Political Science and has worked in radio and television. He is presently Director, Lucknow Doordarshan. His works include two short story collections, *Nae Ahd-Naame ki Saughaat* (1975) and *Mere Hisse ka Zehr* (1997), and a collection of poetry *Beetee Ruton kaa Manzar* (1996), for which

197

he has received several awards from the Urdu Academies of Maharashtra and UP. His latest novel is *Banaraswali Gali*.

RATAN SINGH (b. 1927): Born in Daud in District Narowal, Pakistan, he did a BA from Lucknow University. While he retired as Station Director, Radio Kashmir, Srinagar, he was also editor of *Aaftab-e Jadid*, Urdu daily from Jabalpur and has written several collections of short stories, many of which are included in the textbooks of various state boards. His Urdu collections include: *Pehli Awaaz, Pinjare Ka Aadmi, Kath Ka Ghoda, Gah, Pani Pe Likha Naam*, etc. His autobiography is *Beete hue din*. He also writes in Punjabi.

BAIG EHSAS: An eminent fiction writer and Professor of Urdu at Osmania University and University of Hyderabad, he has also served as Member, Urdu Advisory Board, Sahitya Akademi. Beside editing the Urdu journal *Sab Ras*, he has written three collections of short stories, namely: *Khosha-e Gandum, Hanzal* and *Dakhma; Shor-e Jahan* (critical essays); *Krishan Chandar: Life and Works* (Research), *Shaaz Tamkanat* (monograph). He is the recipient of the Sahitya Akademi Award 2017, including Best Writer Award by Government of Telangana, Lifetime Achievement Award by Telangana State Urdu Academy, among others.

SYED MUHAMMAD ASHRAF (b.1957): Born at Sitapur, a town in the Awadh region in UP, he belongs to a family of devout scholars and Sufi saints of Marehra Shareef, district Etah, UP. Presently posted as Chief Commissioner of Income Tax in Kolkata, he has steadfastly pursued his career as a senior officer in the Indian Revenue Service along with his literary and academic interests. His major work includes two collections of short stories: *Daar Se Bichchre* (1994) and *Baad-e Saba Ka Intizar* (2000)

Notes on Contributors

for which he received the Sahitya Akademi Award; and a novel *Numberdar ka Neela* (1997).

DEEPAK BUDKI: A Kashmir-born short story writer, critic and a researcher known throughout the contemporary Urdu world for his stories encompassing human behaviour, both individual and collective. A post-graduate in Botany and a bachelor of Education, he also attended a coveted course at the National Defence College, New Delhi besides becoming an Associate of Insurance Institute of India, Mumbai. He was a member of Indian Postal Services from where he retired in 2010. For almost nine years he went on deputation to the Army Postal Services. Budki has six collections of short stories, one collection of mini stories, four collections of critical essays and book reviews besides a well-researched book titled *The Non-Muslim Short story Writers of Urdu*. His short stories stand translated into English, Hindi, Kashmiri, Gojri, Marathi and Telugu. Several scholars have written dissertations on his life and works for obtaining M Phil and Ph D degrees from various universities.

HUSSAINUL HAQUE: Born in Sasaram, he retired as Professor and Head of the Urdu Department of the Magadh University in Bodh Gaya. With his first short story published in 1966, he has subsequently written over 200 storied published in six collections: *Pas-e Parda-e Shab, Soorat-e Haal, Ghane Jungalon Mein, Matla, Sooi ki Nok Per Ruka Lamha, Neo ki Eint*; and three novels, namely, *Bolo Mat Chup Raho, Furat* and *Amawas mein khwab*. He has received the All-India Sohail Azimabadi Award from Bihar Urdu Academy, the All-India Literary Award from Bengal Urdu Academy, among others.

ZAMIRUDDIN AHMAD (1920): Born in Fatehgarh (Uttar Pradesh), he migrated to Pakistan in 1947. His stories are redolent with references to the life he had known in India. Along with Naiyer Masud and Abdullah Hussein, he is counted among the post-realist writers of the Urdu *afsana* who came after progressive upsurge. Having worked as a journalist with APP, BBC and the *Dawn*, there is a certain cosmopolitanism in his writing and an easy naturalism.

ABDUS SAMAD: A Professor of Political Science. he began his writing career in 1961 with the children's Magazine *Ghuncha* from Bijnour. His first collection of short stories, *Bara Rangon Wala Kamra*, appeared in 1980 and his first novel, *Do Gaz Zameen*, in 1988. This has been followed by six collections of short stories, eight novels (including one in English), one collection of literary sketches, two books related to Political Science, and two works of translation. He has received the Sahitya Akademi Award in 1990 for *Do Gaz Zameen* and the Bhartiya Bhasha Parishad in 1998 for the same novel. He has received the Ghalib Award for prose in 2014.

RAHMAN ABBAS: Contemporary Urdu novelist and twice winner of the State Sahitya Academy Awards, he is author of seven books including four novels *Nakhalistan ki Talash, Ek Mamnua Muhabbat ki Kahani, Khuda ke Saaye Mein Ankh Micholi,* and *Rohzin. Rohzin* has been translated into German, English and Hindi. The German translation was discussed in Switzerland as part of 'The Days of Indian Literature' in February 2018. This novel has also received the prestigious LitProm Grant managed by the Swiss and German Government. Rahman lives in Mumbai.

SIDDIQUE ALAM (b. 1952): After retiring as Senior Joint Commissioner from the Directorate of Commercial Taxes, West Bengal he now lives in Kolkata. A novelist, short story writer, playwright and poet, he was born in Purulia. He has published three collections of short stories: *Aakhri Chhaon,*

Notes on Contributors

Lamp Jalaney Waley, and *Bain*; two novels *Charnock ki Kashti* and *Chinee Kothee*; a collection of poems *Paththar mein Khudi Huyee Kashti*; as also a collection of short stories under the title of *Nadir Sikkon ka Baks* published in Pakistan. He has also translated the novel *Waiting for the Barbarians* by J. M. Coetzee published in Pakistan by *Aaj*, Karachi, under the title of *Wahshion Ka Intezar*. One of the finest voices in contemporary Urdu fiction, specially for the magic realism ingrained in his stories, Alam is known also as an incisive critic and for his use of innovative and experimental methods as a playwright.

TRANSLATORS

ZARINE JALIL MENON graduated from St .Stephens College, Delhi University and went on to complete her M.A in mass communications from M.C.R.C, Jamia Millia Islamia. She has worked as creative executive in various television and radio concerns including Star TV and Big FM. She is the author of the book *Make Me Happy Salads* and founder of Salad Stories — storytelling workshops for children and parents. She lives in Mumbai.

RAKHSHANDA JALIL is a writer, translator and literary historian. She runs *Hindustani Awaaz* and lives in Delhi.

DAISY ROCKWELL is a painter, writer and translator, living in the United States. She has PhD in South Asian literature and has translated numerous works of fiction from Hindi and Urdu, including Upendranath Ashk's *Falling Walls*, Bhisham Sahni's *Tamas*, Khadija Mastur's *The Women's Courtyard*, and Krishna Sobti's *A Gujarat Here, a Gujarat There* (all published by Penguin India). Her political paintings have been exhibited internationally. www.daisyrockwell.com

TABINDA J. BURNEY is a doctor who practises in London. She has a keen interest in Urdu literature and poetry. She is also an enthusiastic baker and is the author of the award-winning *How to feed your child (and enjoy it!)* by Niyogi Books. She studied at Lady Hardinge Medical College, New Delhi. She grew up and lived in New Delhi before moving to UK. She has previously translated Urdu short stories into English, as part of an anthology titled *Urdu Stories* (Shrishti).

AALIYA WAZIRI has done a BA in Philosophy and is presently studying Law. She has translated this story with Mahjabeen Jalil with whom she has previously also translated from Urdu into English.

HUMA MIRZA has studied English literature from Aligarh Muslim University. She is interested in Urdu and English literature and is presently involved in translating her father Khalil-ur-Rehman Azmi's book, *Urdu Mein Taraqqui Pasand Adabi Tehreek*.

SYED SARWAR HUSSAIN was born in 1955. He taught English at Magadh University, Bihar and Jamia Millia Islamia, New Delhi. At present he is teaching English at King Saud University, Riyadh. His publications include *Ideology and the Poetry of Stephen Spender* and five collections of Urdu short stories translated into English: *Despairing Voices* (2011), *Ashes in the Fire* (2012), *The Eastern Brew* (2013), *Nameless Lanes* (2016), and *Scattered Leaves* (2017).

NABINA DAS is a 2017 Sahapedia-UNESCO fellow, a 2012 Charles Wallace creative writing alumna (Stirling University), and a 2016 Commonwealth Writers Organisation feature correspondent. Born and brought up in Guwahati, Nabina's poetry collections are *Sanskarnama* (2017),

Notes on Contributors

Into the Migrant City (2013), and *Blue Vessel* (2012). Her first novel is *Footprints in the Bajra* (2010), and her short fiction volume is titled *The House of Twining Roses* (2014). A 2012 Sangam House, a 2011 NYS Summer Writers Institute, and a 2007 Wesleyan Writers Conference alumna, Nabina writes and translates occasionally in English, Assamese and Bengali while her poetry has been translated into Croatian, French, Bengali, Malayalam, and Urdu. A guest faculty at University of Hyderabad for Creative Writing, Nabina has worked in journalism and media for about 10 years, and is the co-editor of *40 under 40, an anthology of post-globalisation poetry* (2016).

DAEM (Daem Mohammad Ansary) is a teacher by profession and a budding short story writer and critic. He is presently translating *Charnock ki Kashti*, a novel by Siddique Alam.